Seever Kerns has spent the last fifty plus years as his best friend's subordinate, even though his lion is far more powerful. When he meets Reese Nelson, he realizes the human is his mate and thinks Fate is rewarding his patience. Unfortunately, even though Seever can scent that Reese is attracted to him, the human resists, hiding behind a belligerent façade. Trouble with a rogue shifter soon interrupts his attempts to woo his standoffish mate, and Seever makes a grave mistake. He had assumed that Reese — who was there visiting his cousin, Rocky, a human bonded to a shifter — was aware of shifters and the paranormal world. Reese freaks out, refusing to believe what is right before his eyes. Even Rocky's influence does little to calm him. Can Seever convince Reese that they belong together, or will Reese cut his losses and flee, which would put his human in even more danger?

This book is a work of fiction. Names, characters, places, and incidents either are products of the author's imagination or are used fictitiously. Any resemblance to actual events or locales or persons, living or dead, is entirely coincidental.

Burning the Chef's Buns
Copyright © 2019 Charlie Richards
ISBN: 978-1-4874-2479-4
Cover art by Angela Waters

Published by eXtasy Books Inc or
Devine Destinies, an imprint of eXtasy Books Inc

Look for us online at:
www.eXtasybooks.com or www.devinedestinies.com

Burning the Chef's Buns
Shifter's Regime, Book Three

By

Charlie Richards

Dedication

The three Cs in life: Choice, Chance, and Change. You must make the choice, to take the chance, if you want anything in your life to change.
~Unknown

Chapter One

"The last of the perimeter cameras have been installed," Seever Kerns told his best friend and boss, Councilman Vincentius Goldstein. Leaning against the closed door behind him, he crossed his arms over his chest as he grinned broadly. "I told you I could get it done in three days."

Vincentius chuckled as he lifted his hands in surrender. "You were right." Then his smile turned wry as he swept his gaze over him. "You look like shit, though. Go to bed."

Seever would have laughed, but he was too busy fighting back a yawn. His fellow lion shifter was right. He was damn exhausted, hardly able to stay on his feet. Still, the extra effort was worth it.

I made the damn place safer for the little fliers.

Several months before, Vincentius's systems had been hacked, prompting the councilman to order the hacker tracked down and brought to the estate for questioning. It had been discovered that the man had been a guinea fowl shifter named Cho . . . and he'd turned out to be Vincentius's mate. Seever guessed he'd had to do a bit of groveling at some point, since the little man had forgiven him, and they'd bonded.

Cho wasn't the only one they'd added to their household that day, though. A few days later, the shifter's whole flock and their mates—or those who had them—had arrived. That had been nearly another dozen people.

Good thing this estate is massive.

Many of the new arrivals brought out the protective instincts of the people in security—Seever included. As the head of the household's security, the safety of everyone was his primary concern. Sadly, with the escape of a couple of ex-councilmen and several enforcers going rogue with them, his job had become even more difficult.

Shaking his head, Vincentius offered him a bemused smile. "I really am grateful for everything you do for me, See. Thank you."

"I'm on my way to bed soon. Shower first, though," Seever told Vincentius, pushing off the door. "And you never have to thank me. This is our home and our family."

"I'm glad to hear you say that." Vincentius's brows furrowed as he peered up at him from where he sat. "I occasionally worry, since we both know your lion is quite a bit more dominant than mine, but to outward appearances, you answer to me."

Seever snorted, his lips curving into a wry smirk. "What other people think is irrelevant," he stated, resting his hand on the doorknob. While he really wanted to get out of there so he could enjoy that shower he'd mentioned, he wouldn't walk away from his friend in the middle of the conversation. "We have a system that works, and that's between us."

Vincentius nodded. "I'll start incorporating the cameras into the system right now then."

The abrupt subject change didn't concern Seever. He and the councilman didn't make a habit of sharing their feelings. On occasion, they would talk about their problems over a drink, but that had been before Vincentius had bonded with Cho.

Now I get to shoot the shit with almost a dozen guys as I avoid Prescott's come-ons.

Seever mentally laughed at his thought as he twisted the knob and opened the office door. *Gods, I must be tired.* Smirking, he began exiting the room.

"Oh, hey, Seever," Vincentius called, causing Seever to turn back around. "This afternoon, I heard from Rocky that his cousin is visiting next week."

"His cousin?" Pausing tiredly, Seever rested his forearm on the doorframe. He leaned his temple on it as he eyed his boss, forcing his sluggish brain to focus. "Okay. Uh . . . I'm assuming Rocky gave you his name and shit, so you could run a background check? Get a picture?"

As the head of security to the estate of a man on the Shifter Council, he liked to know who would be wandering around the area. Knowing a person beforehand often headed off problems before they might arise. Plus, if some random dude appeared at the gate that they weren't expecting, it was Seever's job to verify who they were and if it was safe to allow them on the property.

Vincentius obviously recognized Seever's fatigue, for he concisely stated, "Yeah, Rocky said his name is Reese Nelson. I'll forward his picture and information to you." His eyes narrowed as he warned, "Do not start it now. Go get your shower and pass out."

Nodding, Seever silently agreed. "No way I could stay awake right now anyway." Even though he hated to admit to weakness, even to his buddy, he had to share the truth. Pulling his phone off the clip at his belt, Seever checked the time. A little after two in the afternoon. "I can't imagine that I'm gonna wake again today. I'll look at it in the morning."

Giving Seever a thumbs up, Vincentius stated, "The info will be in your inbox when you wake." Then he gave Seever a knowing look as he added, "And I *won't* be sending it for at least an hour, so you won't be tempted."

Seever scoffed. "You know me too well."

With a wave of his hand, Vincentius turned back to his computer systems.

Closing the door, Seever headed down the hall and stopped at a door a short way from the councilman's computer room. He occupied an apartment-like suite on the front side of the home. His boss's—and recently Cho's—set of rooms were on the other side of the hall facing the gorgeous rear expanse of lawns. People who also occupied the other sets of rooms in their wing were Alpha Ashton—the leader of Cho's flock—and his mate, Ranger. Then across from them on the backside was his beta, Gilbert, and his mate, Hess.

The upper floor of the estate's opposite wing that had once been reserved for guests, even though it was rarely used, was now occupied by the rest of the flock and their mates. The lower floors were home to guards and staff as well as a nicely equipped security suite.

Dismissing everything, Seever gave in to his body's needs. He stopped in his closet and stripped his jeans and t-shirt. Once nude, he headed to his ensuite and turned on his shower.

One of the nice perks of living in a fancy estate was fantastic water pressure and several high-end waterfall shower heads. Resting his forearms on the tile, he laid his forehead on his right one.

Seever groaned deeply as he reveled in the hot spray pounding on his exhausted muscles. He'd been awake for nearly forty hours, and his body was telling him he'd overdone it. Still, Seever had needed all those cameras and motion detectors up.

Now, even if a mouse shifter came onto the property while in animal form, their security team would know about it. Of course, that also meant they would be checking out a lot more wildlife, too. Shifters came in all shapes and sizes—from spider to elephant—so their security people were going to become really good at tracking the natural hunting paths of their huge estate's normal animals.

Sadly, that meant being aware that someone could be watching if someone decided to have sex out in the woods.

That thought caused Seever to smile as his thoughts drifted once again to Prescott. The man was a very sensuous wood duck shifter. He had a lean, lithe build, and his pale blue eyes always held a wealth of flirtatiousness.

Seever had never fucked where he lived before, but with Prescott's constant advances and innuendo, he was damn tempted to change that.

Thinking about the pretty man, Seever felt his prick plump a little. Too bad he was too tired to even jack off. Shaking his head, he grabbed his body wash and loofah and got to work cleaning himself.

Don't want to pass out in the shower.

Once Seever had finished scrubbing off nearly two days of sweat, he shut off the water and exited the huge space. He grabbed the towel and began rubbing himself dry even as he left the bathroom. His eyelids slipped closed as his damp feet sank into the lush carpet of his bedroom.

Pausing, Seever swayed as he rubbed over himself. He let out a deep sigh and tipped his head down, then snapped his eyelids back open. Shaking his head, he dropped the towel on the floor and crossed the last couple of steps to the bed.

Seever flopped face-first onto his bed, using the last of his strength to swing his legs onto the mattress. He groaned and stretched before finally succumbing to his body's need for rest.

The sound of a beep roused Seever. Blinking quickly, he struggled to get his eyes to focus. He peered blearily at his nightstand, noticing the time as seven-twelve in the morning. Rolling over, he sprawled on his back and stared at the ceiling . . . then his eyelids slid shut again.

Another few hours of sleep seemed like a fantastic idea.

Except, the insistent beeping sounded again.

"Damn it," Seever grumbled, forcing his eyelids back open. Turning his head, he realized his cell phone was not on his nightstand. "Where the hell did I leave it yesterday?"

Seever swung his legs to the side of the bed and followed the sound. In his closet, he fished under the pile of clothes and found his phone still attached to the holder clipped to his belt. Seeing he'd missed two calls from Willow, his second-in-command in security, he quickly called her back.

"Mister Kerns, I'm very sorry to wake you," Willow stated by way of greeting. She handled the night shift nearly every evening, finishing her shift at seven-thirty. "But I have a stranger at the gate demanding to be let in. He says if he isn't allowed to see his cousin, he's going to call the cops."

"Cousin?" Seever mumbled, crossing to a drawer and pulling out a pair of jeans. "Who's he claiming is his cousin? What's his name?"

"His name is Reese Nelson, and he's supposed to be Rocky's cousin," Willow replied concisely.

"Allow him entrance," Seever ordered, recognizing the name. Except, he was a week early. "Usher him into the lounge. Request coffee. I'll meet him there." After receiving an acknowledgement from Willow, Seever asked absently while grabbing a green polo shirt from a hanger, "Is Rocky up, yet?"

It was barely after seven. Damn early to be calling on someone, but Seever knew the huge body-builder was an early riser.

Must be part of caring for a little one.

"If Rocky is, he, Hector, and their son haven't ventured from their room, yet."

Nodding absently at Willow's response, Seever stated, "I'll check it out."

"Yes, sir."

Seever disconnected the call, then opened his email. He spotted the message from Vincentius and opened it. The picture of a slender, mocha-skinned male in a dark-green polo shirt and form-fitting navy-blue jeans offered a feast for the eyes. Seever took in how the man sported a serious gleam in surprisingly light-brown-colored eyes.

For some reason, Seever wondered what Reese would

6

look like when he smiled, and he felt his blood heat a little at the thought. He shook his head as he scrolled past the picture and did a quick scan-through of the information Vincentius had dug up on him. Reese was a chef at a restaurant in Colin City. He was thirty years old . . . oh, and he was single.

To Seever's surprise, his cat chuffed with pleasure at that knowledge.

Gods, it's been too long since I've gotten laid.

After moving his belt and phone clip to the jeans he currently wore, Seever clipped his phone in place, then he pulled his shirt over his head. He quickly made a pit stop in the bathroom, going through his morning routine swiftly. Skipping shoes and socks, he left his suite and headed toward the lounge. All the while, Seever hoped the staff had already placed that carafe of coffee in there for him.

Just why would a guy say he's coming, then drop in early?

Stopping outside the lounge, Seever rubbed his palms over his face. He struggled to get his brain to engage. Seever inhaled deeply, then let it out slowly. After doing it a second time, he froze as a tantalizing aroma he'd never before smelled tickled his nostrils.

What the hell is that?

His stomach involuntarily clenched, and he rubbed his palm over his abdominals. His heart rate sped up in his chest. Even his blood heated in his veins, and his mouth watered.

When Seever's lion rowled in his mind, and eagerness filled him, a suspicion formed. More than happy to see if he was right, Seever pulled open the lounge's door. He stepped through, closing it behind him.

Seever's gaze was immediately snagged by the slender male standing on the far side of the room. The human's skin appeared a little darker than in his photo, and it seemed to gleam in the sunlight that came in from the window he stood in front of. When the man turned, probably having heard the door, Seever just managed to keep from gasping. The man—Reese Nelson—his light-brown eyes were striking in his lean face.

The light masculine scent—which reminded him of cinnamon rolls and male musk—continued to tease at his senses in a way that drove nearly all intelligent thought from his mind.

Holy fucking shit! Reese is my mate. About fucking time!

To Seever's pleasure, he spotted the way Reese's eyes opened just a smidge. The human's lips parted, and he swept his tongue out to lick his bottom one. Reese's gaze even dipped to linger at Seever's groin.

Unfortunately, then Reese's eyes narrowed, and he opened his mouth.

"Where's Rocky?"

Seever just stayed his natural reaction to lift his brows in surprise upon hearing Reese's combative tone. *Day-am!* His need to soothe his mate quickly flooded him, shocking him with the intensity to make the man happy.

Remembering he had a job to do, Seever fought against his nature. *It won't be long.* He did his best to mentally reassure his annoyed inner animal.

"Probably still sleeping," Seever answered evenly, striding toward the carafe and coffee mugs he spotted on the sideboard. "I know I was." He sent a smirk in Reese's direction, hoping to soften his light scolding. "Coffee?"

"Rocky's an early riser. I know he's up by now," Reese countered, drawing a few steps closer.

Seever poured himself a mugful before coming up with a reply. Since Reese hadn't bothered to answer, he poured a cup for him, too. After opening a single-serving cup of creamer and pouring it into his own mug, Seever picked it up and brought it to his lips, unable to resist taking a sip.

After humming softly, Seever indicated the second cup

he'd poured. "Do you take it black? Cream? Sugar? Half and half?" Seever knew there would be some tucked in the mini fridge hidden in the cabinet beneath the sideboard.

"A couple packets of sugar, please."

Pleased to be making progress—Seever had gotten Reese to share even a tiny thing about himself—he nodded as he put his own cup down and fixed up his mate's coffee.

Chapter Two

Appreciating that he was wearing briefs and comfortable jeans, Reese Nelson fought against the arousal heating his body. He did not *not* want the handsome Caucasian man before him. It didn't matter that Reese thought Seever's big, broad, heavily muscled body was sexy as fuck.

I don't date his kind.

The wonderful flavor of the coffee burst across his taste buds, giving Reese something to focus on other than the handsomeness of the man before him. He took a few steps backward, away from the man who'd greeted him—sort of—and leaned a hip against the back of a sofa. Tightening his lips into a mild frown, Reese pinned his gaze on the stranger.

Reese did his best to ignore the guy's thick black hair. He absolutely did not admire the way it was pulled away from his face in a low ponytail, the style accentuating the aristocratic lines of his face. How the man's whiskey-amber eyes appeared to hold an intense warmth did not cause an answering heat in his chest.

Reminding himself why he'd come early, Reese narrowed his eyes as he met the other man's gaze. "So? Where's my cousin?"

The way Rocky just up and left was even more suspicious than how he'd moved in with his boyfriend of like . . . two minutes acoupla years ago.

Reese just *knew* something was going on with these guys. Had Rocky been taken in by some kind of cult? He never would have thought it of his body-building cousin. The man had always been so level-headed and mentally focused. That was why Reese hadn't been surprised when, even against his parents' encouragement, Rocky had chosen to keep and raise Jayden—his son—when his one-night stand had decided she didn't want him.

She'd been a bitch anyway.

"So, where's Rocky? Who are you? And why are you keeping me from my cousin?"

Reese decided to lay it out bluntly. He needed answers.

"My name is Seever Kerns. I'm the head of security here," the man—Seever—told him, holding out his right hand. "And you are Reese Nelson, Rocky's cousin."

"Yes, I am," Reese replied, taking the man's hand only because it would be rude if he ignored him. As soon as his palm touched Seever's warm flesh, he felt the hairs on his forearm stand on end. Reese squeezed and released quickly—or tried to, seeing as Seever continued to hold his hand. Confused, since the man wasn't squeezing as if in a sign of dominance, Reese muttered, "How do you know who I am?"

Seever grinned widely as he finally let him go. "Rocky told us you were coming, so I got a picture of you on my phone," he stated unabashedly. "We run background checks on any person we think is going to stay here."

His lips curving into a slight smirk, Seever winked at him as he crossed to a chair and sank down in it. He kicked up his bare feet onto the coffee table. Crossing his legs at the ankles, he let out a long sigh before taking another swallow of his coffee.

As Seever pulled the drink from his lips, he waved his free hand to the chair next to him. "Sit and take a load off, Reese," he encouraged. "And I'll tell you why I'm not tracking Rocky down just yet."

Reese opened his mouth, then snapped it shut again when he realized his throat was too dry to get words out. The man stretched out and comfortable was a thing of beauty. Judging by the confident twinkle in his eyes, Reese bet Seever knew it, too.

11

Growling under his breath, Reese moved to the indicated chair and perched on the cushion. He took a swallow of coffee, doing his best to ignore the press of his fly against his straining erection. Clenching his free hand into a loose fist, Reese placed it on his upper thigh in an effort to hide his need.

After clearing his throat, Reese pinned his stare back on the sexy man and stated, "Okay. So?"

"I'll give you an answer first, then ask a question," Seever revealed. "Then you answer. Fair enough?"

Reese scowled at him, annoyed by what he felt was Seever giving him the runaround. Seeing as he didn't think he had a choice, he nodded briskly.

"Good." Seever rested his coffee mug on his flat stomach, drawing attention not only to his cut abdominals but to the hint of skin where his polo shirt was riding up. "So. Your cousin."

Jee-suz! He knows exactly what he's doing.

"If Rocky is awake, he's doing one of two things. Either caring for Jayden or fucking Hector. I'm not going to interrupt either activity. Not unless it's an emergency. Did you come early because it's an emergency?"

Upon hearing the word *fucking,* Reese's brain skittered to a halt.

Fucking. When was the last time I got laid? What would that smooth flesh peeking out between Seever's jeans and shirt feel like? I don't see a treasure trail. Does he have any body hair? Does —

"Reese?"

Realizing where his mind had gone — somewhere where it'd *never* gone before — Reese blinked and scowled at Seever. "What?" he asked, doing his best to ignore the heat that had begun to fill Seever's whiskey-golden eyes. *Gorgeous. Fuck!* Realizing he was about to make a fool of himself, Reese finally registered the bigger man's words and snarled, "No, it isn't an emergency." Narrowing his eyes, he leveled a cold look Seever's way. "Unless checking to make sure family is safe and okay is an emergency."

"Some people would think that it is," Seever admitted before taking another swig of his beverage. "And he is well and happy."

As Seever lowered his mug back to his belly, Reese couldn't help but stare at that strip of exposed skin again.

"Damn, Reese," Seever rumbled, his voice taking on a huskiness that caused goose bumps to form on Reese's arms. "The way you're looking at me—" He paused on a groan as he reached down and adjusted himself.

Reese knew he'd been caught staring, but that didn't stop him from glaring at Seever and his smug expression. Falling back on his default setting—go on the attack—he straightened his spine as he curled his lip. "Fuck you, pal."

His snarled words didn't have the expected effect.

Instead of annoyance, Seever's expression turned . . . hungry. He slowly sat up, and while leaning across the arm closest to him, he swept his gaze over Reese in an open, feral perusal. "Oh, Reese. We'll definitely be fucking, but *I* will fuck *you*." A growl entered his tone as he continued, "And you will *beg* for it, my mate."

Even as arousal surged through Reese, he fought it. He didn't want this obviously dominant asshole, no matter how he pushed every one of his buttons. Ignoring the way his body thrummed with arousal, Reese ground his teeth.

No way do I want the attentions of a white, rich asshole.

Reese had made that mistake before, even if the first time it hadn't been sexual. It had still turned out damn humiliating . . . and the humiliation and bullying had lasted years.

"I'm not your mate," Reese declared, glaring at him. "We're not friends."

Seever's jaw sagged open as his eyebrows shot up. Obviously, Reese's refusal wasn't what he'd been expecting.

Just as quickly, he appeared to gather himself, for he cocked his head and swept a narrow-eyed gaze over Reese.

Then Seever's stomach rumbled.

Humming, Seever slowly rose, his movements sleek and sensual. They kind of reminded Reese of a cat rising from a relaxed position. He rubbed over his belly, sliding his hand under his shirt provocatively.

"Do you want more coffee?" Seever asked ... as if he hadn't just been trying to entice Reese with his hard, strong, oh-so-sexy body. Before Reese could come up with a response, he added, "I'm getting some."

Reese felt his lips part in surprise. The other man's smooth change of subject and completely laidback responses to his attitude confused the shit out of him. Most people responded with equal abrasiveness.

What is Seever up to?

"You sure?"

Hearing Seever's question drew Reese out of his confused thoughts. Maybe he should have taken a day to rest and relax after arriving, so he wasn't so out of it. He'd caught a plane after a long, ten-day work stint with twelve, thirteen, and even fourteen-hour stretches in the kitchen.

Damn asshole boss.

Still, somehow Reese had just felt that he *needed* to get there to check on Rocky.

Now if I could just figure out why.

"Seems you're struggling to focus as much as me, handsome," Seever commented, crossing to him still carrying the coffee carafe. "Right that empty cup of yours."

Acting on instinct, Reese obeyed. When had he finished his coffee, anyway? As he tried to sift through his confused thoughts enough to get them sorted, he watched Seever return to the sideboard, then grab a couple of sugar packets. Those he tore open and poured into Reese's mug.

That was nice of him.

14

Damn it!

Reese scowled as he took a deep swallow of his fresh coffee.

Why am I responding and thinking like this?

"Come on, Reese," Seever urged, beckoning with his fingertips. "I'm hungry. Let's go to the dining room for breakfast." When Reese hesitated, Seever smirked as he waggled his brows and beckoned with his fingertips again. "Before too long, your cousin will wander in. We don't stand on ceremony at breakfast. Everyone straggles through eventually."

Since seeing the inner workings of the home was his goal, Reese nodded. "Okay." But he didn't take Seever's hand. Instead, he placed his free hand on the cushion and pushed off of it, slipping to the left and around Seever's body. Standing once again, Reese was reminded of just how much bigger the man was—six-foot-three of solid muscle.

Seever lowered his offered hand, only to turn and rest it on Reese's lower back. Tension surged through him, and he stepped forward. Except, Seever followed.

"Relax," Seever urged, his words almost sounding like a purr. "Come this way, handsome."

Then Seever pressed a little harder even as his fingertips teased over his spine, causing goose bumps to spread over Reese's flesh. A burst of tingles trickled up and down his spine. Reese even felt the zings in his tailbone, making his groin warm, his cock twitch, and his asshole clench.

Reese wanted to pull away, but since he didn't know where he was going and Seever walked just a half-step behind him, he couldn't.

Manipulative bastard.

Even as the thought flitted through Reese's mind, his blood continued to heat and his arousal surged. He couldn't remember the last time he'd felt so out of control. Reese just didn't understand why.

Wait a sec. Did Seever slip something in my coffee? An aphrodisiac of some kind?

But how? I watched him pour it. And he drank some, too . . . and he wasn't the one who made it.

Reese was so lost in thought that he barely registered the gorgeous décor and beautiful marble floors of the stately formal dining room. Once they'd passed the table, he glanced back, taking in the huge ornate table that seated eighteen. When Seever stated, "Through here," with his hand still urging him forward, Reese returned his attention forward.

Upon pushing through the swinging door, Reese swept his gaze over the area. He took in a much more intimate dining area — still large, seating six, with huge floor to ceiling windows which let in the morning sunlight. To the right was another swinging door, and it was being pushed open.

Seever's grip suddenly changed from encouraging him forward to grabbing his hip to stop his forward movement. Reese glanced at the man as he stepped past him, the move subtly putting Seever in front of him. If Reese didn't miss his guess, it was almost a protective move.

But why?

Reese shifted his attention to the people entering the room. Both were young men — maybe in the early twenties range. The first man had blond hair and blue eyes, was slender, and appeared handsome in a boy-next-door kind of way. His eyes rounded as he froze, halfway to the table, as he took in Seever and Reese.

The second man had medium-brown hair and tanned features. His frame was just a little on the plump side, and he had a pair of glasses perched on the edge of his nose. He paused, too, then grinned.

"Mister Kerns." The brunette sounded surprised to see him, and his cheeks took on a pinkish hue. "Good morning, sir."

"Good morning, Ezekiel," Seever replied. Tipping his head just a little, he added, "Who's your friend?"

Using one of the plates he carried — one in each hand — Ezekiel indicated his . . . friend. "This is Lorian Jackson." He swallowed hard enough to cause his Adam's apple to bob even as he began moving again, crossing to the table. Ezekiel used a bump of his elbow against Lorian's upper arm to get the blond to do the same. "He's my boyfriend."

"Ah." Seever's lifted one brow as he commented, "Here early. Got big plans today, boys?"

Hearing the boys comment, Reese wondered not only how old Seever was, but if he'd been wrong about the young men's ages, too. As Reese watched, Ezekiel's cheeks darkened even further. It wasn't until they were settled at the table, a plate of food in front of each of them — and the same with the drinks that Lorian had been carrying — that Ezekiel mumbled his response.

"He stayed the night."

After an instant's hesitation, Seever snorted and rolled his eyes. "Got it." He started moving again, urging Reese toward the swinging door the pair had come through. As he passed Ezekiel, he patted him on the shoulder. "I ain't your parents, kid." Then he winked and reached around Reese to push the swinging door open for him.

Reese entered the kitchen, and all thoughts of Seever, Ezekiel, and his friend flew right out of his head. Sucking in a sharp gasp, he swept his gaze over the huge, spacious kitchen. It had three refrigerators, a double oven, more counter space and cupboards than he'd ever seen outside of a restaurant, and there were high-end finishes everywhere.

"Oh, that's right," Seever murmured, rubbing his back to get Reese's attention. "You're a chef. What do you think?"

"Just damn," Reese murmured, starting forward. He ran his fingertips over the granite countertop to his right, admiring the smooth, dark surface. "Any chef would be lucky to work in a place like this."

Chapter Three

Seever's heart thundered in his chest upon hearing the awe in Reese's tone—and if he wasn't mistaken, he scented a hint of envy in his mate's scent, too.

I bet I can work with that.

"I've never really thought about it," Seever commented softly as he watched Reese admire the spacious area. "Our chef is Ezekiel's mother, Marian, so maybe you and her can swap recipes." Crossing to the fridge on the left, he asked, "Remind me where you work?"

Seever had still been half asleep while skimming through Reese's file. Besides, now that he knew the man was his mate, he would much rather have Reese share with him of his own free will.

While waiting for a response, Seever reached into the refrigerator and pulled out a baking dish containing a ham, potato, and cheese casserole. He placed it on the counter, giving the fridge door a hip-bump to close it. Next, he crossed to a cupboard and grabbed a pair of plates.

"You're hungry, right?" Seever clarified, doing his best to ignore the rumble of his own stomach. Not eating anything for nearly a day would do that to a shifter. He offered a wry smile Reese's way as he set down the plates. "It would be rude to eat in front of you, after all."

Reese's attention returned to Seever. His gaze flicked to the food he was dishing onto the plates. "Yeah, I could eat." He leaned his left hip against a counter and crossed his arms over his chest. "I work as the head chef at *Southwestern Bar & Grill*. It's a reasonably nice place, but the hours are long, and the owner can be—" Reese snapped his mouth shut.

Seever guessed he probably hadn't meant to complain about his job. He figured it was the mate-pull affecting him.

Sharing with one's mate was a natural side effect. Appreciating that it was already starting to affect his stubborn human, Seever grinned.

"I suppose no job is perfect." Seever chuckled softly as he shrugged. "Hell, I'm head of security here, and I can think of a few annoying aspects to my job, too."

Reese smirked, one dark eyebrow arching.

"Ah, want examples?" Seever recovered the casserole dish with the plastic wrap and picked it up. "Well," he began slowly, thinking quickly as he reopened the fridge. "Every once in a while, hours can be a bitch, especially if I receive a threat against the councilman." Rolling his eyes, Seever snorted. "Which, unfortunately, is often."

Cocking his head, Reese narrowed his eyes. "Councilman?"

Seever shoved the plates into the massive microwave. "Yeah," he replied easily. Once he'd started the food heating, he turned and grinned at Reese. "You're standing in the home of Councilman Vincentius Goldstein. You knew that, right?"

"Uh—" Reese scowled as his shoulders tensed.

"Oh."

I guess not.

Seever wondered why Rocky wouldn't have explained to Reese that Vincentius was a shifter councilman. Maybe he didn't bother going into details about the shifter world, since his cousin wasn't mated to one—or hadn't been at the time Rocky had moved.

Perhaps Rocky intended to share all that once Reese was out here.

Wondering such things wasn't getting him anywhere.

"Well, in our world, the council monitors the behavior of—" Seever began slowly, choosing his words carefully.

"Hey, Reese!" Rocky's booming voice filled the kitchen. "What the hell are ya doin' here, cuz?" The huge black male strode across the kitchen and wrapped Reese in a one-armed hug. Rocky held Jayden in his other. Grinning broadly, he rocked back and forth a few times, then released Reese. "Great ta see ya!"

Reese's smile turned rueful as he shrugged his slender shoulders and straightened his polo shirt. "Well, I had to come and make certain that you were well." Reese glanced from Rocky's face, then between Seever and Hector, and finally back to Rocky. "Living with a councilman? What's that all about?"

Rocky's eyes widened, and his thick lips parted.

The man's obvious surprise confused Seever. Furrowing his brows, he again tried to find the right words. "Didn't you explain why your flock had to move out here? Cho being mated to a shifter on the council and all?"

"What did you say?" Reese asked cautiously.

At the same time, Rocky shook his head as he blurted out, "Seever, he doesn't know."

Seever gaped.

Oh shit! How did I miss that?

Seever really should have read the file thoroughly. Of course, he'd been told that Reese wasn't expected until next week. Between his lack of sleep and the pull of the mate bond, Seever's brain was true and completely addled. His common sense had gone right out the window.

Sliding his gaze to Reese, Seever opened his mouth, then closed it again.

Reese's eyes narrowed, and he scowled as he peered around the room. "What the hell are you all talking about? I don't know about what?" His eyes widened for an instant before his lips curved into a sneer. "This is a cult, isn't it?"

"No. Absolutely not," Seever quickly denied. "I—"

The sound of raised voices in the dining room drew Seever's attention.

"—ruining our species!"

"Lorian, stop! What are you doing?" Ezekiel cried, telling Seever who had spoken.

"Die!"

Acting on instinct, Seever shifted even as he lunged for the kitchen door. Between one heartbeat and the next, his lion filled the area, leaving his clothes shredded. Good thing it was a swinging door, otherwise, his massive beast would have burst right through it.

Seever took the chaos in at a glance, then leaped into the fray. He grabbed the nape of the cougar shifter he didn't recognize, yanking it off Vincentius's just finished shifting body, and threw it across the room. The tawny feline shifter's body crashed through the center window, disappearing from sight.

Upon hearing a cry of shock from the direction of the kitchen, Seever froze. He recognized the sound of his mate in distress. Movement in his peripheral pulled his attention back to the councilman, who was rising to his paws. Underneath him was Cho, still in human form.

Blood dripped from claw marks on Vincentius's back.

Fucking hell!

Attacking a councilman without cause was damn near a death sentence . . . and Seever was standing there giving the perpetrator the chance to get away.

Seever yanked his head out of his ass—mentally speaking, anyway—and leaped through the broken window. To his left, he spotted the flash of a tawny-colored tail and gave chase. With adrenaline spiking through his veins, Seever dug his paws into the thick grass, surging forward.

It didn't take Seever long to get within striking distance. Just as he pounced, the other cat shifter turned and swiped at him. Seever twisted in midair, dodging the strike. The other shifter rolled and tried again, but Seever was quicker.

Lunging at his hind end, Seever snapped his jaws around the cat's haunch. He used his forward momentum to twist the other shifter around. As expected, the animal lost his balance and toppled.

Seever took advantage. He let go of the cat, watching the slender beast roll. Judging its movements, Seever timed his leap. He wrapped his jaw around the other shifter's throat and squeezed, sinking his teeth through the thick fur. The tang of blood hit his taste buds before the other cat stopped moving.

The smaller animal whined, and Seever growled. The cat did his best to roll and show his belly. Easing his hold, Seever backed up a step.

The cougar immediately jumped to his feet and began sprinting away once more. Seever took two steps, then paused as a massive tom turkey swooped down in front of the cougar, raking his talons across his ruff. The beast twisted away but was met by a large gray and auburn striped tabby — a Scottish wildcat.

Thad and Lachlan.

Seever shifted. By the time he had the ability to speak, Thad's turkey had landed on the cougar's back and was drawing blood with his talons. Lachlan's cat had wrapped himself around the shoulders of the larger feline, and his canines were tearing into his neck.

"Guys, stop," Seever shouted, holding up his hand. "I need the asshole alive."

Thad gobbled indignantly even as he hopped off the cougar's back end. Strutting around the beast toward his head, he gave the cat what could only be called *the evil eye* as he continued to warble. Lachlan, on the other hand, Seever could see that he'd relaxed his jaw, but he didn't let go.

Good.

Sometimes having help was invaluable, and the mated pair who'd arrived were lethal when necessary and one-hundred-percent dedicated to the safety of the flock living at the estate.

Which is why I love having them here as enforcers.

"Shift now, cougar." Seever thundered the order as he stalked toward the trio. "Do it, or I'll have Thad peck your tailbone."

In response to his words, Thad lowered his head, spread his wings halfway, and began running toward the cougar's back end.

The cougar immediately began to shift. His change was impressively swift, taking only about fifteen seconds. The average shifter took nearly double that, so this cat had either been practicing or was far more dominant than he'd originally come across in the dining room.

Once the young blond male lay prone in the grass, Seever didn't miss the gleam of hatred filling his blue eyes. Still, he had to ask, "Is Lorian your real name?"

The man didn't respond. Instead, he glanced at the cat still threatening his neck.

"You can release him, Lachlan."

After letting out a low growl, Lachlan obeyed. He only slunk backward one step though. Baring his teeth an inch in front of the shifter's face, he let out a low, snarling hiss.

Seever fought back a smirk. The ex-council enforcer and ex-investigator was damn fierce. Due to his size, much smaller than a cougar or lion, most people underestimated him.

It was a mistake they only lived to make once.

"Now then," Seever commented, crossing his arms over his chest. "Name?"

The young man curled his lip but still didn't answer.

Seever smirked. "Oh, you'll change your mind soon enough." Stepping forward, he grabbed the man's upper arm and jerked him to his feet. "I've had the pleasure of enjoying many, many interrogations." Seever waggled his brows as he forced the cat shifter to begin moving back toward the estate house—Thad and Lachlan flanking them.

"But since Lachlan joined our ranks . . . well—" Humming, he finished, "Lachlan has a certain *zeal* when it comes to finding out the truth, you see. He *loves* making his mate happy, and his mate's primary concern is the safety of everyone here."

Chuckling low in his throat, Seever saw the way the guy's skin lost its color, and his expression blanched. "Ah, you caught on, have you?" Leaning close as they walked, Seever purred into his ear, "He's happy to do whatever is necessary to protect this place. Sure you don't want to do this the easy way?"

"I can tell you where Councilman Krakow is hiding out," the shifter blurted out.

"Really?" Seever pretended disinterest as he exchanged a glance with the shifters still in animal form. "How interesting. I can't wait to hear all about it."

In truth, the information could prove useful. The ex-councilman Paraben Krakow was on the run with ex-councilman Sasha Delaney. They'd taken half a dozen high-ranking enforcers with them. Fortunately, three of them had already been either killed or captured, and a fourth was discovered to be a spy—Nkosi.

Too bad they hadn't heard from him, yet.

Seever knew he had to be patient, since only two days before, Vincentius and Cho had finished setting up the system Nkosi needed for communication.

"I can tell you their plans, too," the cougar shifter claimed.

Inhaling deeply, Seever discovered the slight tinge of acridness on the air. He hid the revelation that he knew the cougar was lying.

Little shit. Why does he think he can get away with this?

"Are you going to tell me your name, then?" Seever asked, curious to see if the turnaround would get him any truthful answers.

25

"Cabo," the cat shifter replied. "But I'm not comfortable telling you my last name."

Huh. That scented at truthful.

"Why not?"

Cabo glanced fearfully at their companions before admitting, "If I'm punished after I explain why I had the right to go after Councilman Goldstein, I don't want you all going after my family, too."

Hmm . . . that sounds ominous. What the hell is he hiding? Or is he really just concerned about his loved ones?

Seever had no idea, but seeing as Cabo was talking—"So why did you go after the councilman?"

To Seever's surprise, a low snarl erupted from Cabo. "I want to say it to his face," he snapped, his anger making his toned body vibrate.

Ooookay. What the fuck?

When the back patio of the estate came into view, Seever eagerly swept his gaze over the area. He spotted Vincentius, Cho, and Ezekiel flanked by Willow, Cassidy, and Beakner—his second-in-command plus two guards. Even Ezekiel's parents were there—Marian and Nero—lending their son support.

Conspicuously absent, however, was Reese, Rocky, and Hector.

Where the hell is my mate?

Seever not only recalled Reese's wail of distress, he remembered Rocky telling him that his mate didn't actually know anything about shifters. *Gods, I've completely freaked him out.* Rocky probably had him holed up somewhere and was desperately trying to soothe him.

"Mister Kerns, where do you want me to take this traitor?" Willow asked bluntly as she stepped forward, the guards flanking her. "A cell or the interrogation room?"

"I deserve to have my case heard by the asshole who wronged me!" Cabo cried, jerking forward and nearly pulling from Seever's grip.

Damn it, man! Focus!

Yanking Cabo back, Seever snarled, "Watch your tongue, Cabo. You'll get your chance."

"Cabo?" Ezekiel spoke up. He had his arms crossed, gripping the opposite upper arms in his palms. His face was pale, and his eyes gleamed behind his glasses. "Y-You lied about your name?" Ezekiel's breathing hitched, and a tremor went through his body. "Is everything you said a lie? E-Everything b-between us?"

Unfortunately, Cabo just rolled his left shoulder in response, not even offering him a glance.

"Why?"

Seever fought back a wince, knowing he wasn't the only one who heard the pain in Ezekiel's voice.

"So I could get close to Goldstein," Cabo declared, his expression hard, his anger brimming through him. "That was the only thing that mattered!"

"You used me," Ezekiel cried, anger filling his voice. "I demand restitution!"

"Why?" Cabo snorted as he finally focused on Ezekiel with a sneer on his lips. "Because I fucked you? You begged me for it!" He rolled his eyes as he shook his head. "I did you a favor."

"Why you—" Ezekiel leaped toward Cabo, his body rippling as he began to shift.

Fortunately, Cassidy caught him before he'd finished and began carrying him away, kicking and screaming. Opossums weren't normally vicious animals, but they could be damn wily and had plenty of sharp teeth. Ezekiel's mother followed behind, peering over her shoulder at Cabo—*and damn, if looks could kill.* Nero cast concerned glances his family's way even as he put the finishing touches on bandaging Vincentius's back.

"That's enough!" Councilman Goldstein hollered, pulling

away from Nero and the last of the bandage he was attempting to apply. "What is your damn beef with me?"

Cabo curled his lip as he stated, "You promised my sister you'd mate with her, then you turned out to be a fag!"

"Good grief," Vincentius grumbled. "Take him to the cell. I'll talk to him there."

Seever gritted his teeth even as he handed Cabo over to Willow and Beakner. The man fought for an instant, then Lachlan let out a snarling hiss, which caused him to settle.

As soon as Cabo had disappeared into the house, Seever turned to Vincentius. "Are you well, sir?"

"Well, enough," Vincentius stated, tugging Cho into his arms. "Thank you for pulling the fucker off me." He scowled in the direction of the doors. "Asshole went after Cho."

"Our mates can be considered our weak spot." Seever turned a slight smile Cho's way. "No offense."

Cho nodded, his eyebrows pinching. "I'm not a fighter. I get it."

"And speaking of mates, I need to go see mine." Seever started toward the door. "How'd he take the revelation of shifters?" He grimaced as he pulled open the door. "I didn't realize he wasn't aware of them until Rocky told me."

"Wait," Vincentius called, making him pause. "You found your mate? Who? When?"

Right. I haven't told anyone, yet.

"Rocky's cousin Reese showed up early," Seever explained. "He's my mate."

Vincentius's eyes widened, and his lips curved into a huge grin. "Congratulations, See! That's fantastic!" Then he must have noticed what Seever did, his mate's pensive expression, for he said, "What is it, hon?"

Cho appeared damn nervous, shifting uneasily from foot to foot, and it took him a few seconds of nibbling on his lower lip before he answered. "I-I don't mean to speak ill of anyone"—he stared at Seever from beneath his lashes—

"especially a mate." After another heartbeat of silence, Cho whispered so low that even with Seever's shifter hearing, his words were tough to make out. "Reese is, um, h-he's kinda bigoted . . . against white people, especially if they're rich."

For an instant, Seever felt anger surge through him upon hearing such accusations being cast against his mate. Then he forced himself to recall his interactions with Reese. The man's belligerence made sense.

Well, shit.

Heaving a sigh, Seever nodded. "Somehow, I'll get through to him." Then he turned and headed into the house.

"Good luck," they both called.

Seever nodded and waved without pausing or glancing back.

Somehow, I think I'm gonna need it.

Chapter Four

"What the hell is going on, Rocky?" Reese shouted when his cousin had finally finished propelling him into some kind of sitting room. He whirled, swinging his arms wide in frustration as he added, "What the hell did I just see?"

When Rocky hesitated, his brows furrowing and uncertainty filling his expression, Reese took a second to glance around. From the toys on the floor, he bet it was part of Rocky's suite that he'd mentioned weeks before on the phone. His cousin had claimed to be living in a suite of rooms bigger than most apartments.

"Damn it, Rocky! What?"

Resting his hands on his hips, Reese glared at his cousin. Seeing the way the other man hunched his shoulders, clutching Jayden close to his chest, not to mention how Hector clung to his side, rubbing and soothing his arm, Reese's temper flared. He wanted to know what the fuck was going on around there.

No way did I actually see what I thought I saw.

"At first, considering the level of weird arousal I was feeling, I was sure I'd been slipped some kind of aphrodisiac." Reese crossed his arms over his chest as he tried to puzzle it out. "Except, then in the kitchen . . . no." Reese shook his head. "Definitely a hallucinogen. What the fuck could produce both responses?"

Scowling at his cousin, Reese demanded answers. "Is this what happened to you? You felt shit and saw shit that couldn't possibly be real?" Deciding that had to be it, he nodded. "Detox. We'll find a clinic and get our blood drawn so the doctors can help us clear whatever shit they're giving us out of our systems."

"Will you shut the fuck up for two seconds so I can answer any of the million questions you just asked me?" Rocky barked, clearly frustrated. When Jayden began to fuss, he handed him off to Hector. "We might be loud, baby. Will you take care of him in the bedroom?"

Even as Hector took Rocky's son, he nodded while saying, "Kitchenette first, though. He hasn't had anything but his bottle and needs a solid snack."

Rocky's expression could only be called adoring as he bent and pecked Hector's lips. "Thank you so much, my mate."

As Hector rushed from the room, taking a squirming, whining youngster with him, Reese found his attention snagged on that one word. "Mate? What's that mean?" Gaping at Rocky, Reese hissed, "Is that how they suck you in? Seever called me that. Said he was going to fuck me and just expected me to go along."

Spotting the way Rocky's jaw sagged open, Reese realized what he'd just admitted. His face heated, and he prayed his light-brown cheeks hid that fact. Reese cleared his throat as he tried to remember what else he'd intended to say.

He didn't get the chance.

Rocky grabbed his upper arm and asked, "Seever called you his mate? When? What *exactly* did he say?"

Even as Reese struggled to recall the words, he shook his head. "Oh, no. You told me to shut up, so you could answer my questions." He jerked his arm away, then crossed both over his chest as he frowned up at his cousin. "So?"

Heaving a deep sigh, Rocky rubbed his hand over his bald head. "In the kitchen, remember when Seever mentioned shifters?"

"Good grief." Reese rolled his eyes. "Yes, I recall." The pieces suddenly snapped into place in his mind. "Wait a second." Lifting a hand, he snorted as he shook his head.

"You don't really think what you saw was a man turning into a lion, do you?" Reese barked a laugh upon seeing Rocky's serious expression while he nodded. "I told you! That's *not* possible. We had to have been slipped a hallucinogen or something." After glancing over his shoulder toward the doorway that Hector had disappeared through, Reese returned his focus to his cousin. "Gather up Hector and Jayden, and we'll find a nearby clinic." He shooed with his fingertips. "Hurry. Before any of those security guys get back."

Rocky shook his head. "It's *not* hallucinogens, Reese. There really *are* paranormals living right here beside the humans. Shifters, vampires, gargoyles, and more." Scowling, he rested his hands on his hips. "I never really thought you had such a crazy imagination."

Rearing his head back in surprise, Reese took a step backward. His heartbeat spiked in his chest, and his breathing accelerated. Sweat broke out on his skin, and he rubbed at his temple.

"I-I'm not the one with the imagination," Reese mumbled, shaking his head again. "You're . . . they —"

"Slow your breathing, Reese," Rocky urged. In the next instant, he rounded Reese and rested his huge hands on his shoulders. As Rocky massaged Reese's shoulders, his touch was gentle. "Inhale deeply, Reese. Come on, man. Focus."

Reese tried, but black spots began to dance across his vision. He swayed and couldn't stop it when he found himself being eased onto a sofa. His head pounded, and someone pushed his head between his knees.

"Keep breathing, Reese." Rocky's deep voice barely penetrated the fog surrounding Reese's mind. "Be right back."

Then the hand on the back of Reese's neck disappeared. The desire to pop up, find the nearest door, and run away from all the craziness pulsed through him. Except, when he tried to stand, his legs shook.

"Hey, you're okay, Reese." Seever appeared before him. He wore only a pair of sweatpants, putting his broad, gorgeous chest on display. "Just sit back down, my mate. Everything will sort itself soon enough. You've just had a shock."

Reese found himself staring, his focus riveted on the tan nubs surrounded by a dusky-skinned areola. His mouth watered, and he licked his lips. Even as Reese obeyed the press of Seever's fingers and eased back onto the sofa cushion, he felt his blood heat in his veins. His prick once again thickened just from Seever's presence.

"Well, that scent is definitely better than panic." Seever knelt before Reese and cradled his jaw in one hand. "Meet my gaze, Reese."

Once again, Reese obeyed the gentle press of Seever's hand, and he met the man's gaze. He spotted the smile straight away and admired the sensual curve of his lips. Reese found himself attempting to lean forward, wanting to taste them — so plump and perfect.

"Reese, babe," Seever murmured, his voice husky. "As much as I want to do all the things your scent and hungry expression are calling me to do, I think you need to accept facts first."

Reese blinked, then jerked backward, pulling his face from Seever's grip. Lifting his hand, he placed it on the man's shoulder and pushed. As soon as the big, sexy, dark-haired man toppled onto his butt, Reese leaped to his feet and bolted toward the door.

No way did Reese want to stay in this nut-house for a second longer. He didn't understand what was going on, but he didn't like the loss of control he experienced. Never had he felt tempted to —

"Whoa there," Seever cried just as his arm snaked around Reese's waist and jerked him to a stop. "Can't let you go, yet, either, hon."

Reese felt Seever's strong frame pressed against his back, the man's heat blanketing him and warming him. A tremble worked through him, and he shivered. He didn't know when he'd grown so cold, but he suddenly felt a desire to snuggle back against the man and soak up not only his attentions, but his heat, too.

"Wh-What's going on?" Reese was too confused to feel bad about the slight tremor in his voice. He spotted Rocky between him and the door and realized that, even if Seever hadn't grabbed him, he wouldn't have been able to leave. "Am I"—he swallowed hard—"a prisoner here?"

"Not a prisoner, Reese," Rocky assured, lifting his hands in placation. "We just can't let you leave until you accept a few things." His thick lips curved into a wry smile. "And until you're a little calmer, huh? Can't drive while in your state."

Reese knew Rocky was right, but that didn't mean he had to like it.

"Feeling a little better, babe?" Seever asked huskily.

That was when Reese realized Seever was nuzzling his cheek against the side of his neck. Not only that, but Reese was tilting his head so he could give the man more room. Maybe it had something to do with how soothing it felt. It could also have been how distracting and arousing the feeling of Seever rubbing his palm over his abdominals felt—even through his shirt.

"You're petting me." Reese furrowed his brows upon blurting out the words. "Why does being around you, being touched by you, distract me so much?"

Reese gripped Seever's wrists, then pulled the man's hands from his body. Stepping forward, he eased away from him. He turned and lifted his hands. Facing Seever, Reese swept his gaze over the sweatpants-clad man.

"Why are you wearing sweats? What happened to your jeans?" Reese glanced at Rocky, then slowly rounded Seever and headed back to the sofa. His mind was going a mile a minute, processing everything he'd seen and heard in the last hour, and his legs were beginning to feel like jelly. "Th-This isn't a cult?"

Reaching the sofa, Reese gripped the arm for support as he slowly lowered himself onto a cushion. He watched as Rocky started toward him slowly, almost as if he feared spooking him. Seever stayed where he was, resting his hands on his hips, although he focused on Reese with what could only be called a hungry intensity.

"So, okay." Rocky eased onto the sofa a few feet from him and rested his curled fingers on his thighs. Rubbing his hands over his jeans, Rocky held his gaze. "Are you ready to accept the truth now?"

Reese glanced between the pair but couldn't stay focused on Seever. The way the man looked at him was just too damn distracting. He nodded while holding Rocky's gaze.

"So, the short and quick explanation, since Seever looks like he's ready to jump your bones." Rocky waggled his brows playfully, which did nothing for the heat Reese felt filling his cheeks. "Like I mentioned before . . . shifters, vampires, gargoyles, and more. Most of the paranormals at this estate are shifters, although there is a vampire guard here, too." Rocky waved his hand as if dismissing the comment. "Anyway. A shifter can change into a certain animal at will. Whatever you might have seen on those cheesy movies, forget it. They don't need the full moon, obviously, since you saw Seever change in the kitchen, and they're completely cognizant."

"I-I'm not sure what that means," Reese admitted,

movement from Seever's direction catching his attention.

Seever settled on the coffee table a few feet in front of Reese. "That means, even when I'm in my lion form, I will still know who you are and what you mean to me."

Reese fought back a shiver upon hearing the huskiness in Seever's voice. Swallowing hard, he muttered, "What I mean to you?" Clearing his throat, Reese straightened and frowned at the man. "We just met. We don't mean *anything* to each other."

As Reese watched, Seever's cheeks flushed and his eyes narrowed. "Actually —"

"*Actually*, that's another thing about paranormals," Rocky swiftly cut in.

After seeing the way Seever cast an annoyed look Rocky's way, Reese focused on his cousin. "What?"

God, am I believing this? Paranormals? Shifters?

Except, Reese realized he sort of had to. He'd seen it happen after all. As much as he would love to cling to the idea that he hadn't truly seen what he had thought he'd seen, Rocky was right. He didn't have this kind of imagination.

"Paranormals live a long time. Shifters can live upward of five hundred years," Rocky told him slowly. "They have super-fast healing, better senses. Are stronger and faster. But it can be a long time to be alone."

It was obvious that Rocky was choosing his words carefully, seeing as he kept glancing from Reese to Seever and back again. Plus, he had that tightness around his eyes and lips that Reese knew Rocky got each time he had to share difficult news. He'd seen it when Rocky had come out, when he'd shared his intention to be a body-builder, and when he'd told of his decision to keep Jayden and raise him alone.

"I'll say," Reese murmured, hoping to urge Rocky to continue.

Rocky cleared his throat, glanced Seever's way once more, then leveled a serious stare on Reese. "Fate offers each paranormal a soul mate. Shifters and gargoyles simply call him or her a mate. A vampire calls it a beloved, and"—he paused and waved his hand—"not important. Anyway, once a shifter finds their mate, they bond with that person, entwining their life threads." Rocky grinned suddenly, his dark eyes gleaming with happiness. "Hector is my mate. My other half. And we'll live for centuries together."

Centuries! Holy shit!

"Fountain of youth," Reese whispered before gaping at Rocky. "A-And you're okay with, with living so long?"

"With Hector by my side, absolutely," Rocky confirmed. "He makes me happy, content, feel loved." He sighed, sounding dreamy. "He completes me."

Just as quickly, Rocky sobered and pinned a hard stare on Reese. "On the flip side, that means you can't share the existence of paranormals with anyone. It could endanger your mate. My own mate and his friends were experimented on by scientists. Secrecy for safety is everything, Reese."

"Experimented on?" While Reese didn't understand Rocky's attraction to the bouncy twink, he would never do anything to jeopardize the happiness his cousin had found. "That's terrible. Yeah, yeah." Reese already began nodding as he tried to reassure Rocky. "I'll never tell anyone."

Besides. Who would believe me? Well, other than evil assholes who want to take advantage of their gifts?

"Back to how Rocky and Hector are mates," Seever prodded, drawing Reese's attention. His whiskey-amber eyes appeared to almost glow with his desire. "Shifters recognize their mates by scent. When Hector scented Rocky, he pursued him, and after Hector claimed Rocky, binding their lives together, your cousin immediately moved in with Hector. The instinct to stay together is undeniable." Pinning Reese with a hungry grin, Seever stated, "*You* are *my* mate,

Reese. That means we will do the same."

Shock flooded Reese, and he straightened as tension spiked through his shoulders. He glanced at Rocky, searching his face for denial. His cousin sported a wince, telling him that he believed what Seever had stated.

Gulping, Reese shook his head. "No."

"Yes," Seever immediately countered, narrowing his eyes.

"Blunt," Rocky muttered, shaking his head. "I was trying to ease into it, man."

"Couldn't wait," Seever replied. "Finding our mate is a time for celebration." Then he grinned widely as he added, "And the lust definitely affects our brain, making us impatient."

"I think," Reese whispered, blinking hard as he struggled to process everything. "I think I'd like to lie down."

Unable to stay focused, Reese didn't fight it when the dark spots descended, his eyes rolling to the back of his head.

A little mental quiet seemed like a damn good idea right then.

Chapter Five

Staring at Reese tucked into the guest room's bed, Seever leaned against the doorframe. "Your cousin . . ." Seever allowed his voice to trail off, uncertain what he wanted to ask.

"How's he taking this?" Rocky guessed. He stood a few feet away, leaning against the wall outside the room.

Seever sighed, then nodded once.

Rocky lifted his shoulders in a brief shrug. "He's . . . going to adjust eventually, but" — waving his hand in the air, he twisted his lips into a grimace — "it could take some time." Meeting Seever's gaze, Rocky admitted, "This is way out of his wheelhouse, as the saying goes."

Snorting softly, Seever returned his focus to his sleeping mate. A frazzled Doctor Cooper had assured him that the man had dropped from shock . . . and maybe a little fatigue. Evidently, his mate worked too damn hard.

Hopefully, I'll be able to change that.

"What human would ever have *accepting paranormals* as something in their *wheelhouse*?" Seever lifted one hand and made air quotes.

Rocky met his gaze and smirked at him. "A guy who loves werewolf and vampire stories and movies?"

Seever chuckled softly, nodding. "All right."

Pushing away from the wall, Rocky told him, "If he wakes up and you want help, just holler." He patted him on the shoulder. "I know you must be eager." While his dark complexion hid Rocky's mild embarrassment, Seever could scent it as he told him, "I understand the desire to finish the bonding process."

Nodding again, Seever murmured, "Thank you."

After grunting in response, Rocky headed out of the

room.

Seever appreciated his offer of help. Having family or friends available to help ease a human into the paranormal world was damn useful. Otherwise, it could take a lot longer.

Of course, if Seever had known that Reese hadn't been aware of the paranormal world, he would have approached the man completely differently. Lack of sleep had definitely addled his brain. He bet the fact that he hadn't gotten laid in so long had accentuated his need, too.

Absently listening to the door open as Rocky left the suite—the rooms were in Seever's wing near his own—he thought of the man's earlier advice. He had planned to lay Reese in his own bed. He had hoped that being surrounded by Seever's scent would help relax him and accept him all at the same time.

Sadly, Rocky had warned him against that plan. He'd shared his concern that if his cousin woke there, he might feel manipulated or forced. Waking in a comfortable, neutral setting would be much easier on his mind.

Seever had acquiesced.

Upon hearing Vincentius asking Rocky for an update, Seever turned away from the gorgeous view. He had things to do, after all. Even though Seever knew that his friend would give him time off to woo his mate, Seever wanted to check up on a few things before doing so—mainly, Ezekiel.

The young shifter had to have been feeling used and maybe even a bit degraded. Plus, Seever had to admit he was a little curious about Cabo's accusations. While he was certain they were completely unfounded—hell, Vincentius had never hidden his sexuality even before he'd mated with Cho—his assertions were extremely odd.

Stepping into the hallway, Seever shut the door quietly behind him. "Hi, Councilman," he greeted with a smile.

"Thank you for checking up on my mate."

"Of course." His fellow lion shifter grinned. "I can't wait to meet him."

Rocky tipped his head in a nod, then excused himself.

"The doctor said he's resting comfortably," Vincentius commented. "And Rocky said you didn't realize Reese wasn't aware of shifters, and I know you shifted in front of him to help me." He rested his hand on Seever's shoulder and squeezed companionably. "Again. Thank you."

"I could respond that it's my job," Seever teased, grinning at his friend. "But instead I'll say, you're my friend, and if possible, I will always help."

Vincentius grinned even as his amber eyes twinkled. "And the fact that you walked away from your confused mate makes me appreciate it all the more."

Seever chuckled softly, unable to come up with a response to that. Drawing away from Vincentius's comforting hand, he used the same move to touch the other shifter's shoulder and urge him to turn, too. When Seever started walking, Vincentius did the same.

"Have you talked with Ezekiel and his parents, yet?"

Lifting his left brow, Vincentius peered at him questioningly. "Doc Cooper saw to your mate. Didn't he say anything to you?"

Hearing the hard edge in Vincentius's tone, a fissure of unease slithered through Seever. "No. He didn't say anything." He hesitated, then added, "While he seemed annoyed, I just put it down to what happened." Seever spotted his friend's wince. "Not the case?"

"Right or wrong, Marian and Nero are placing the blame for what happened with Ezekiel and Cabo squarely at my feet." Even as Seever's jaw sagged open with his shock, Vincentius continued on a growl, "Sure, they blame Cabo, too, but Marian reminded me that if I weren't involved with a feud with other powerful shifters, then those around me wouldn't become a target."

Growling low in his throat, Seever demanded, "Did she say anything else?"

"Only that with the increase in security, it was coming to feel like they were prisoners in their own home."

"Damn it. This protection is to keep everyone here safe," Seever snapped, jabbing his pointer finger at nothing as he spoke. "If their son had followed the rules and hadn't snuck his *boyfriend* in, this wouldn't have happened."

Vincentius lifted his hands in a gesture that spoke clearly of his own frustration. "I know, and I mentioned that, but you know Marian when she's in Momma Bear mode."

Seever sighed deeply. "I know."

Anytime something happened to either Nero or Ezekiel, Marian circled the wagon, so to speak. She'd cared religiously for her son when he'd broken his arm at the age of thirteen. When Nero had been harmed by an injured shifter he was treating, Marian had refused to allow her husband back in the room unless the patient was restrained.

Seeing as Nero was their only doctor on hand, Seever had seen to it that it was done... even when the shifter had apologized.

"I'll go talk to them," Seever stated, fighting back his own frustration. "I have to reprimand Ezekiel for bringing in a stranger unannounced. Then I'll go from there."

Vincentius winced. "Marian isn't going to like that."

Seever scowled at the councilman. "Vincentius, I don't give a shit. His desire for sex put not only you in danger, but also your mate and every other person who lives here."

While Vincentius grimaced, he did nod.

"What about a report from Lachlan, yet?" Seever asked curiously. "I haven't seen anything emailed to me, but I thought that may be due to the fact that I found my mate."

Vincentius nodded. "Yeah. I'll forward it to you." As they walked, he did just that. They parted ways at the central hallway with Vincentius adding, "Good luck."

Glancing back at the councilman with a smirk, Seever nodded. "Thanks."

While Marian was an opossum shifter and he was a lion, Seever still didn't look forward to dealing with her.

Hoping to avoid the situation altogether, Seever stopped at Ezekiel's suite and knocked on the door. The man had moved out of his parents' rooms almost five years before, after he'd turned twenty-two. The move had been expected by Seever and many others, even though Marian had done her best to talk Ezekiel out of it.

When Seever didn't get a response, he called, "I'm using my override code and entering, Ezekiel." Then he did just that. There was a keypad to the left of the doorjamb of each room. Only half a dozen people in the house knew the override code, and all of them would never use it if it wasn't an emergency.

A shifter bringing a danger into our midst is definitely an emergency.

Seever entered the suite. The smell of sex, sweat, and male musk still permeated the rooms. He wrinkled his nose as he winced before crossing to the window off the breakfast nook attached to the kitchenette and threw open the window.

From the lack of noise, Seever already knew Ezekiel wasn't in the rooms. He exited just as quickly, pulling the door closed behind him. After taking in a deep breath of reasonably fresh air, Seever sighed deeply.

So much for the easy route.

Seever reached their suite of rooms half a moment later. He quickly knocked, then crossed his arms over his torso. It wasn't until then that he realized he still hadn't bothered with more clothes.

Oh well.

The only one who might be bothered was Nero since he was human.

The door opened, and Seever found himself staring into the angry eyes of Marian Cooper.

Seever decided it would be best to go on the offensive. "Marian, I need to see Ezekiel." Upon seeing her lips pinch, her expression of denial obvious, Seever added, "This isn't a request, Marian. Let me in."

Marian harrumphed, but she opened the door wider and stepped backward. "Come on in, Seever," she stated, irritation filling her tone. "But you can save your breath. It doesn't matter what you have to say."

"Marian, Ezekiel is an adult in shifter terms, so you know that's not your call," Seever told her forcefully. "He must be held accountable for his actions."

"Oh, you mean how he was targeted because of something Councilman Goldstein did?" As Marian spoke, she picked up a picture off the mantel and took it to the sofa. She began wrapping it in packing paper. "Yes, I've already spoken to him about that. It wasn't his fault." After placing the wrapped picture into a half-filled box, she rested her hands on her hips and glared fiercely at Seever. "None of this was Ezekiel's fault."

"It *is* Ezekiel's fault that a man no one in security knew about was freely eating breakfast when the councilman and his mate showed up," Seever reminded her, doing his best to keep his voice even. "If Ezekiel had followed procedure, he would have known that Cabo wasn't who he said he was, and this entire situation would have been avoided."

Marian blew out a rude noise as she grabbed another picture from the fireplace mantel. "Yeah, right. What young man wants to tell his love interest, *oh, sorry, but in order for you to come over, I have to run a background check on you.*"

Seever growled angrily, glaring at her. "It's the rules for a reason, Marian, and what happened this morning reinforces that."

"What about *your* mate?" Marian asked haughtily. "Did you do a background check on him?"

"Not me personally, but yes," Seever revealed. "Even though Reese is Rocky's cousin, he was still checked. No exceptions."

Marian smirked and shook her head. "And Pete?"

Seever's cat growled in his mind, and he had to agree. He was getting damned tired of Marian's insolence. Still, he drew on the deepest dredges of his patience and kept his tone evenly modulated.

"As soon as the councilman made the decision to bring Pete to the estate, he contacted me, and I started a background check," Seever explained.

The tiny human had been attacked by his neighbors, and only Lachlan and Thad's intervention had stopped something serious from happening. Once Pete had accidentally learned about shifters, Vincentius had hired him as the estate's personal mechanic. He currently lived on the property and loved his job.

"Marian love, stop mouthing off to Seever," Nero ordered as he strode into the front room, carrying a suitcase. He set it down next to the sofa and wrapped his arm around Marian's shoulders, then faced Seever. "I already talked to Ezekiel, and he did apologize. It's going to be a moot point anyway, because we're leaving."

"Leaving?" Seever glanced from the box that he finally realized Marian had been packing to the suitcase on the floor. "Shit, guys. That's not necessary." Lifting his hands in placation, Seever scrambled to think up some way to get them to stay. "We understand what happened was a fluke. I just need to remind Ezekiel of procedure, then it'll be forgotten."

That was how it worked on the surface, anyway. On the down-low, Seever would have one of their best trackers keep an eye on Ezekiel for a few weeks. That way they could confirm that the issue wouldn't become a pattern.

"We understand that, sir," Nero responded respectfully. After a quick glance at a still annoyed-looking Marian, he lowered his voice and murmured, "It has to do with embarrassment as well as a few other things. We'll be leaving this afternoon."

Seever spotted the firm glint in Marian's eyes and knew there was no way he was going to be able to change her mind. Sighing, he nodded before offering, "If you need a reference"—he glanced between them, realizing what the estate was about to lose like a kick to the stomach—"for either a chef or your healing skills, just ask. And I'll be certain to have a severance put together for you, too."

"That's not necessary," Marian countered. The anger and irritation had finally bled out of her voice. She blushed as she added, "We were talking about moving anyway, and we know we're leaving you in the lurch, but this was the final straw, you see."

Fighting back a sigh, Seever instead chose to nod once. "If you don't mind shooting me an email letting me know what the other problems were, I'd appreciate it." He forced an understanding smile to curve his lips. "After all, I wouldn't want to lose others if it's something that I can fix beforehand."

Seever guessed it would be family related, which he knew he couldn't do much about, but he had to make an effort. After receiving confirmation from them both, he turned and headed toward the door. When he reached it, he paused and turned back to face the pair.

"You will all be missed." Seever glanced between them. "You know that. Right?"

"Thank you, sir," Nero replied. "As will you and many others here."

After offering a goodbye and best wishes, Seever exited and closed the door. He didn't allow his sigh of disappointment to escape until he'd reached the end of the hall. Pausing, he scrubbed his hands through his hair and scratched at his scalp.

Seever felt a fatigue headache coming on, and he desperately wanted to go lie down next to Reese.

How would he feel if he woke up with me wrapped around him?

Even the thought caused his blood to swiftly heat and head south.

Oh, and my mate is a chef! Hopefully, we'll still be eating good. Hope he gets along with Thad in the kitchen.

Just as that thought made him smile, Seever spotted Cassidy jogging toward him.

Now what?

Before Seever needed to voice the question, Cassidy told him, "I'm so sorry, sir. Beakner told me to track you down since you don't have your phone on you."

"It's fine. What is it?"

Damn. It must still be in the kitchen with the remainder of my clothes.

"It's your mate."

"My mate?" *What the hell?* "What about him?"

"Beakner's monitoring the cameras right now, and he spotted him on them." Cassidy's cheeks took on a pinkish hue, and he dipped his chin in respect. "He's attempting to sneak out the service entrance."

"Oh fuck no," Seever snarled as he began sprinting toward a side entrance.

I'm gonna tan his hide.

Chapter Six

Reese peered through the branches and mentally groaned. There was a guard at the side gate, too. He wondered if he could find a way to distract him, so he could slip through.

On the other hand, maybe if I stroll right out the door as if I own the place, he won't bother stopping me.

Deciding to keep that as option B, Reese glanced around for a stick or rock or something he could throw to distract the man. He scowled, coming up empty. Reese lowered to his hands and knees, so he could peer even deeper under the beautifully manicured bushes.

Just damn! How could a yard not have one damn rock in it?

Whoever the gardener was should be commended by his boss. Reese, however . . . Reese wanted to smack him upside the head. After crawling along the bushes for a good twenty feet, Reese finally found a stone.

Reese barely bit back his shout of triumph as he grabbed it up. Still crouched on the toes of his shoes, he pivoted . . . and fell back on his ass. He peered up and up, his gaze snagging only an instant on the tan, pebbled nipples on display, and met the gaze of Seever Kerns.

"And just what do you intend to do with that?" Seever asked, pointing at the rock in Reese's hand. "Attacking one of the guards carries a heavy penalty. Not a good way to make friends."

As much as Reese would love to rub his palms over Seever's gorgeously cut abdominals, he glared at the man, instead. "I'm not here to make friends," he spat indignantly.

"Ouch." Seever cocked his head as he rested his hands on his hips. "You have a smart mouth on you, Reese. I'm kinda about two minds on it."

Gaping, Reese stared wide-eyed at the man.

Seever groaned and palmed his dick through his sweats. "Fuck! Don't tempt me!"

Reese spotted the thick erection tenting the crotch of the fabric and snapped his mouth shut. His cheeks flushed, and he hoped his blush didn't show on his skin. Yanking his gaze back upward, he managed to snap his mouth shut again, all the while fighting his urge to lick his lips.

Growling low in his throat, Seever gazed at him as he continued to rub his crotch. "I told you we would fuck, Reese, and I definitely look forward to you sucking my dick." Reaching out, Seever traced the backs of his forefingers along Reese's jawline as he purred huskily, "Perhaps while *I'm* sucking your dick and preparing your ass for my taking. Have you ever been fucked bare, my mate?"

A shiver worked down Reese's spine even as a shudder racked his body. Goose bumps broke out on his chest as the hairs on the nape of his neck stood on end. His cock throbbed, and pre-cum leaked from his twitching dick.

Oh, holy fuck.

Unable to help himself, Reese pressed the heel of his hand to the base of his fly. He groaned even as he shook his head.

"Yes," Seever countered, stepping closer, then bending his knees. "Definitely yes."

Seever's knees hit the ground to either side of Reese's thighs. Bending at the waist, he grinned as he pressed close. On instinct, Reese sprawled backward to get more room, but Seever just kept coming, levering over him.

His back hit the ground, and he struggled with how he ended up in such a position.

Right. Gotta talk.

"Stop it." Hearing how hoarse he sounded, Reese swallowed hard, then tried again. "What the hell are you doing?"

49

"I think it's past time that I kissed you, Reese," Seever stated, revealing that his voice was rough, too. "I want to taste you, my mate, and it will soothe my nerves since I found you trying to run away." His eyes narrowed as a low growl escaped him. "Why did you run?"

Except, Seever didn't wait for an answer. He dipped his head and captured Reese's mouth. The man didn't wait for an invitation, he nipped at Reese's bottom lip and demanded entrance.

Reese gasped in surprise, and Seever took complete advantage.

Seever thrust his tongue into Reese's mouth as he slid his palm under his head. Cradling his skull, he urged Reese to tip his head a little. As he did that, Seever lapped along Reese's tongue, delved deep into his mouth, and teased along his gums and teeth. The man mapped him with a single-minded intensity that caused the hairs on Reese's arms to lift and heat to surge through his body.

Reese groaned into the other man's mouth, unable to stop himself from responding. Mewling softly, he delved his own tongue into Seever's mouth, doing his best to give as good as he got. He teased along the other man's tongue, tasting him, reveling in his masculine flavor.

Breathing huskily through his nose, Reese refused to break the kiss. Never had he experienced anything that caused his nerve endings to fire through him. He felt as if his body was strung tight, his senses singing and his balls throbbing.

When Reese felt the telltale tingle at the base of his spine, he groaned and jerked his head to the side. He hissed a breath, his stomach clenching as he struggled to control himself. His throbbing erection pressed against Seever's own, and he knew that if he just rocked up once or twice, he could be coming, flying high on the release of endorphins.

Reese wanted that so damn badly, but he refused to come in his jeans like some adolescent.

"Oh, Reese," Seever hissed against his ear. "The smell of your arousal is exquisite." He nipped at Reese's earlobe, causing him to cry out sharply, before growling, "What a wonderful sound. Bet you taste even better. Can I suck your dick until you spill your seed in my mouth?" Seever licked a stripe up the side of his neck before adding, "I want to taste you everywhere."

Trembling underneath Seever's broader frame, Reese tried to pull some sort of rational thought into his head. Except, the other man—the man who wanted to be his lover—had driven every sensible notion right out of his head. His body was a fiery mess of need and desire and want.

"Y-Yes, please," Reese uttered, all thought to consequences gone.

"Mine," Seever rumbled, sounding exceedingly happy. He pecked a swift, hard kiss to Reese's already kiss-tender lips, then began scooting down his body. As he did so, he continued to mumble. "Mine. All mine. Waited so long . . ."

Before Reese could even attempt to figure out a response to that, a question, a comment, anything, Seever made quick work of Reese's fly. When the restrictive fabric gave way, his dick thrust upward, seeking freedom, even through the underwear he wore. In the next instant, that was gone, too, and the cool morning air brushed across his sensitive, swollen length.

Reese moaned huskily, shifting restlessly on the grass. With bated breath, he stared down at the top of the other man's head, his face obscured by the way his dark hair hung loosely around his face. It was so damn sexy, and Reese watched, anticipation making his thighs clench.

Then Seever rested his weight on one of his hands and

used the other to push his hair behind his ear. He peered up at Reese through his lashes and held his gaze. Then, *finally*, he lowered his head and wrapped his lips around Reese's crown.

At the first feel of Seever's silky mouth around his head, Reese couldn't stop the moan. He let it out on a long, low breath. The heat of his mouth and wet nudge of his tongue sent a jolt straight to his balls. Reese wanted to spread his legs wide and buck up, shoving his erection deep into that wet inviting cavern, but between his pants and Seever's weight on his legs, he couldn't.

That didn't stop him from trying to thrust. He dug the back of his head into the grass and twined his fingers into the dirt. He arched his back and thrust.

To Reese's surprise, Seever shifted off of him a little, allowing the move. The bigger man opened his mouth and sank deep — so deep. Reese felt his crown nudge the back of Seever's throat, and when the man moaned, Reese barked a harsh cry.

His balls tightened. His gut clenched. When he sank back to the grass, Seever followed him down. Then the man eased back up, sucking harshly, only to do it again . . . and again . . . and —

"Oh, fuck!"

Reese screamed, his body shuddering and twitching. His orgasm crashed across his senses like a rogue wave, sweeping him under. He moaned and writhed in time with the spurts of his seed up his cock. The gentle suction to his crown and the light massage to his frenulum caused the sensations to go on and on.

As the haze of endorphins pinging through his system began to ease, Reese struggled to catch his breath. He panted harshly, his head swimming. Warm tingles still trickled through his system, causing residual pings to dance across his senses.

"Gods, you taste even better than I thought," Seever rumbled huskily. "And the noises you make, the feel of your skin, the weight of you on my tongue." He rubbed his chin over Reese's hip. "Gonna do that often."

Reese managed to focus on Seever, finding that the man stared lazily up at him, a satisfied smile making his whiskey-brown eyes gleam. Opening his mouth, he prepared to offer to help the other man get off . . . except, the rustle of footsteps on grass reached his ears.

Seever immediately jerked onto one elbow, using his second to reach down and adjust his sweatpants. Then he leaned over Reese's groin and glared in the direction of the offending noise. His cheeks darkened to a harsh shade of pink.

Had they been watched?

The idea flitted through his mind, chased by another one.

Did Seever open my pants just to flash my dick at others? To put me on display?

It felt as if someone had dumped a bucket of ice water over his head.

Did Seever use me?

"Get off me," Reese demanded, uneasiness filling him.

"Hush," Seever ordered, glancing his way. Then he frowned toward the noise again. "By all the gods, I swear if you don't walk away this instant, I will pull your balls out through your asshole!"

Reese gaped. His gut clenched. *Ouch!*

"Fucker," Seever grumbled after a moment. When he turned his attention back to Reese, his expression eased into a sheepish look. "I'm sorry, babe. I should have thought about the fact that our grounds are so closely monitored." He slid his hand under Reese's shirt and petted his stomach rhythmically, obviously attempting to soothe him.

"Y-You didn't, um—" Reese paused, nibbling his bottom

lip uncertainly.

"Didn't what? Come?" Seever grinned broadly as he waggled his brows. "Oh, I came. Your seed tasted amazing. Just about blew my balls off."

Reese barked a laugh even as he shook his head. The lethargy from a great orgasm began to creep up on him. Still, he had to be sure.

"While I'm glad you came, that's not what I meant."

"Then what, babe?" Seever continued to pet his stomach as he pressed a kiss to Reese's opposite hip. "Talk to me."

Knowing he couldn't find out if he didn't ask, Reese blurted out, "You didn't put me on display on purpose? For other people to see and rid —"

Reese didn't get to finish the word.

Seever launched up his body until Reese was pinned beneath him. "No one sees you in passion but me," he declared, his expression possessive and feral. "If anyone else does more than look long enough to realize they should walk away and then do so, I will tear their eyeballs out through their ears."

Grimacing, Reese whispered, "Your visuals are kinda . . . gross."

Chapter Seven

Seever blinked, surprised by Reese's response. Struggling to contain the flood of jealousy his mate's comment had unwittingly created, he swept his gaze over his new—and forever—lover's furrowed brows and pinched expression. Between the man's continued scent of unease and the residual traces of annoyance he felt from realizing someone had seen at least some of their activities, Seever was having a damn difficult time enjoying the aftereffects of his release.

Sucking Reese off, hearing his cries of delight and feeling his body move, had quickly brought his own arousal to new heights. He'd barely had enough presence of mind to shove the front of his sweats down. One stroke and the taste of Reese's cum on his tongue had sent him over the edge.

Finally, Seever's sluggish mind processed Reese's words . . . or rather, he parsed out what his concerns actually seemed to point to. Sliding his right hand across Reese's forehead, he teased across his eyebrows. His move eased the man's crease lines a little, and Seever smiled.

"I *am* sorry that we were crept up on, Reese, and possibly some of what we were sharing was seen by another," Seever told his wary human. "If I ever find out who it was, I'll smack him upside his head for his indiscretion, then remind him why he should have kept walking."

To Seever's surprise, Reese snorted. "*His* indiscretion? *We're* the ones who lost our heads and decided to, um—" Reese paused, his dark cheeks managing to reveal just a hint of pinkness.

Seever grinned, then dipped his head and pressed his lips to Reese's. He'd intended it to be a short peck, just a chaste meeting of lips to reconnect. Too bad the second their mouths touched, Reese opened to him, and Seever couldn't resist enjoying another long, thorough taste of his mate.

His mind drifted in a pleasant haze as Seever slid his tongue along Reese's. He relished the taste of man, coffee, and a unique flavor that had to be all his mate's own. It was damn intoxicating, and he couldn't seem to get enough.

He also loved that Reese immediately kissed him back, using his tongue to duel and tease his own.

When breathing became a necessity—and his cock throbbed once more—Seever broke the kiss and let out a groan. "By the gods," he rumbled huskily, taking in Reese's kiss-swollen lips and deeply flushed face. His man's eyes were widely dilated, and he panted for each breath. "You are so fucking stunning. Never dreamed Fate would give me a man as breathtaking and perfect as you."

Reese tipped his head. "Fate?" Then his brows furrowed. "Right. You and Rocky said something about Fate giving you a companion. How does she decide?"

Seever groaned as he eased up, then shifted to a kneeling position next to his human. When Reese immediately went to cover his still-exposed groin, he gently batted his hand away. Then he began to gently do up the fly himself.

"Lift your hips, babe," Seever ordered, which he immediately did.

His mate's seemingly easy response pleased Seever, until after he'd finished doing up his fly and he glanced at his man's face. Reese's lips were pinched a bit, and he was staring toward the bushes to the right. Disliking that uneasy, embarrassed expression on his mate's face, Seever reached up and slid the backs of his fingertips over his jawline.

To Seever's relief, the move drew Reese's attention.

"Are you okay, Reese?" Seever asked gently.

Reese glanced away as he cleared his throat, but a second later, he met Seever's gaze again. "Never had anyone dress me after," he muttered, clearly unsettled.

"Then your prior lovers were inconsiderate assholes. *I* will enjoy every opportunity to take care of you," Seever replied easily with a grin. He rose to his feet and held out his hand. "Come on. I'll see if I can answer your questions." Recalling their prior conversation, Seever added, "And I'll explain a little about shifter dynamics so you'll understand why the other guy was being the rude one and not us." He finished that with a wink.

Reese didn't appear convinced, but he took Seever's hand and allowed him to pull him to his feet.

Seever once again pecked a kiss to his lips—he just couldn't resist—but that time he managed to keep it short. "When we say Fate chooses our mate, it's both accurate and misleading." Wrapping his arm around Reese's waist, he started them back toward the house. "We would have been attracted to each other regardless. All Fate does is heighten our natural responses to each other—attraction, arousal, the need to touch and taste and pleasure. That sort of thing." Seever glanced Reese's way, waiting for his nod. Still seeing a hint of confusion on his mate's face, he added, "That heightened attraction gives the paranormal the heads up that the person in question is the other half of their soul." Seever dipped his head and rubbed his lips across Reese's temple before murmuring, "And it helps the human in the pairing overcome their . . . trepidation regarding the secret of paranormals or other . . . hang-ups from past bad experiences they might have gone through."

Reese lifted his brows as he repeated, "Hang-ups?"

Nodding once again, Seever offered a few examples. "An abusive boyfriend. A cheating boyfriend. A liar." Hesitating a second, he decided to be blunt and offered, "Being used, abused, or made fun of by someone white?"

Tensing, Reese glared his way. "Rocky told you," he grumbled as he tried to pull away.

Seever tightened his hold, refusing to allow his man to put distance between them. "I don't know any specifics, but I was warned that you were a bit . . . bigoted toward white males." He kept his tone light and calm, hoping to keep Reese's ire to a minimum. "Especially if they seemed to be rich." After just a second of hesitation, Seever added, "And it wasn't just from your cousin. It seems your . . . hang-ups"— he cast a wink Reese's way—"are quite well known amidst his flock."

"Busybody assholes," Reese snarled.

"A little," Seever conceded, then he squeezed Reese's side. "But they only do it to try to help."

Reese heaved a deep sigh, but he didn't respond.

Seever took that as a win. His mate wasn't countering or fighting with him, and he seemed calm and was no longer running. Turning his attention to Reese's other comment, Seever thought about the best way to answer.

"In regards to the issue of indiscretion," Seever began slowly. From the corner of his eye, he noticed Reese focus on him with his eyebrows raised. Seever began to realize his mate did that often when interested or questioning. "When someone finds their mate, it spreads like wildfire through whatever shifter group he or she is associated with. It's an unspoken rule that the couple be offered privacy and the time to figure out their bond. If—"

"Wait. Bond?" Reese cocked his head, and his expression turned vacant. "You mentioned bonding once before, too." His lips curved into a wry smile as he met Seever's gaze. "I may have been a basket case when we had that talk in Rocky's room, but I do recall everything. I just didn't really give it much thought until now." As Reese finished his words, he hunched his shoulders and shook his head. "God, is all this really real?"

Seever knew doubt would creep in on Reese at odd times.

His uncertainty didn't concern him. Instead, he found it reassuring. It meant Reese was processing.

"It is real," Seever reassured before bussing another kiss to Reese's temple. "But I understand your hesitance to believe. The secret that paranormals exist is very closely guarded. It's second only to the rule of *never try to come between mates.*" Growling softly, Seever grumbled, "Unfortunately, there is bigotry even in the shifter world, and there are people out there who would say that Fate pairing the same sex is wrong or doesn't happen, and those who claim it does are faking it or lying about it."

Scoffing, Reese muttered, "There are assholes all over."

Seever nodded. "So, to answer your question, if someone walks by and spots a couple in an intimate embrace, the proper action would have been to keep going." He scowled as his thoughts again strayed to what he would like to do to the asshole. "Watching is rude."

Then another thought struck him. "Aww, fuck."

Reese froze, missing a step. "What's wrong?" He even glanced around warily.

Shaking his head at his loud outburst, Seever rubbed up and down Reese's side. "Sorry," he muttered, although he couldn't wipe his scowl from his face. "I forgot about the increase in cameras. Don't worry. I'll—"

"Cameras?" Reese jerked in his hold, then twisted to the side. The move was so unexpected that Seever released him. "We were fucking *recorded*? Asshole!" Reese pointed his finger at him and demanded, "Why? So you can show your friends? So you can—Fuck!" Rubbing both palms over his scalp, he muttered, "This is why I don't trust you people. You always have some ulterior motive. Want to be in control, manipulate and—"

Seever lost his ability to follow Reese's train of thought about halfway through his mate's angry rambling. Still, he caught the gist of it. His mate had been hurt, and whatever pain had been caused, it still festered and ran deep.

Even though irritation filled him that Reese would automatically lump him in with whoever had harmed him in the past, he tried to be understanding. He—

"Oh, hell no," Seever grumbled. "Screw this."

As Reese had been talking, he'd been backing further and further away. Seever lunged and grabbed his human's arm. A quick tug caused Reese to stumble forward and up against Seever's chest, right where he wanted him.

In my arms.

Seever wrapped his hand around Reese's nape and dipped his head. Slamming his lips onto his mate's, he thrust his tongue between them and into his mouth. Seever delved deep, teasing, lapping, and nipping, urging his mate to respond.

Hearing Reese's groan of surrender, feeling him sag in his arms, Seever growled with pleasure. He continued to enjoy his mate's mouth for several more seconds, then he eased the kiss to an end. Seever lifted his head, then nipped his plump bottom lip before pulling away enough to focus on his man.

"Whatever the fuck you were thinking, please stop, Reese," Seever murmured softly. "I didn't plan for a video, and even if one was made, the only ones who would be watching it is us." He couldn't suppress a groan at the idea of watching his mate's face in the throes of passion. "All other copies will be deleted. Like I told you before." A growl entered his voice that he couldn't quite suppress. "Anyone who sees you but me will be punished."

Reese swallowed hard enough to cause his Adam's apple to bob. His nostrils flared as he searched Seever's face. His jaw worked, and he seemed to be struggling.

Seever waited, returning Reese's gaze, giving him a few seconds since he was back in his arms.

Finally, Reese nodded. "I-I'm not certain why, but I believe you."

"And that is just an example of how the mate-pull, the desire to bond and twine our lives, helps ease fears and build a connection." Seever slid his other hand up and down Reese's spine, wishing he was feeling skin, that they were both naked, horizontal, and in his bed. With his right hand, Seever slid it around his mate's neck so he could tease along his jawline, relishing the feel of the smooth brown skin under his thumb. "I will never cheat, never wish for another, and I will devote my life to your happiness and safety." Dipping his head so his mouth rested near Reese's ear, Seever whispered, "Now that I've found you, you are my everything, Reese."

A shudder worked through Reese's body, and Seever grinned. "Now you're beginning to understand, aren't you?"

Reese sucked in a harsh breath, and he shivered even as he nodded once. Then he tipped his head back and met his gaze. His brows were furrowed, and his light-brown eyes appeared troubled.

"Every time you pull me into your arms," Reese began slowly, pausing to lick his lips. "Your touch is comforting, but your words are troubling."

My words?

Seever tipped his head, staring deep into his human's eyes. "My words are of devotion. How are they troubling?" That certainly hadn't been what he'd been expecting.

"Because you expect me to drop everything and stay with you." Reese sighed deeply as his gaze slid downward, and he appeared to be focusing on Seever's shoulder. "I saw it happen with Rocky. I didn't understand at the time, but now I get why he did it."

Sighing deeply, Seever used his thumb to tip Reese's head back up, so their gazes met. "Reese, if I could move to wherever you are, I would do it in a heartbeat, but it would be . . . difficult."

"You mean near impossible." Reese's expression turned wry. "I remember what you told me. You're the second-in-command to a councilman on the Shifter Council. That's damn important." Shrugging, Reese continued, "And I'm a chef. I can get a job in most large towns."

Seever didn't like the way Reese was speaking about his job, even if he did love the fact that his mate was talking about their future. Hell, his man had been running from him not an hour before. It occurred to him that he didn't understand the change.

"Two questions before we go in and shower," Seever stated. "First, we lost our cook this morning because of that asshole who used her son to gain entrance. The job is yours if you want it, and I hope you do." Lifting his hand to stall Reese's response, since he'd opened his mouth, Seever leveled a serious gaze upon his mate. "Second, what changed your mind? An hour ago you were running away."

Reese curved his lips into a cheeky smile before quipping, "Would you believe because you give the best damn blowjobs in history?"

A rusty chuckle erupted from Seever's throat even as he shook his head. "No. Try again."

I need the truth.

Chapter Eight

Reese tried to come up with a response that made sense. The trouble was, he wasn't entirely certain himself. There was something about Seever that called to him, but there was more to it than that.

Something inside me, too.

"I could try to fob it off on your Fate ideas," Reese started slowly, trying to sort his still-churning thoughts. "But you'd probably see through that. Just like the blowjob jest." Smiling, his cheeks heating, Reese admitted, "Although you do give amazing head."

Hell, I came so hard from just his mouth, what will happen when he gets his dick in my ass?

Seever grinned smugly, his eyes gleaming with a hint of wickedness. It was almost like the man could read his thoughts.

Clearing his throat in an attempt to get his mind back on track, Reese rolled his eyes. "Look, part of the reason I came out here was, and I'm not proud of it, and if you tell Rocky, I'll deny it, but—" He grimaced, realizing he wasn't making sense. Shaking his head, he muttered, "I was jealous. There. I said it."

Seever tipped his head, his expression one of thoughtfulness. "Jealous?" His brows furrowed. "Because you were attracted to Hector?"

Even as Seever said the words, Reese felt the way his hands tightened on him. He barked a laugh and shook his head. While Reese wasn't certain why knowing Seever was jealous filled him with, well, pleasure, it did.

"No, absolutely not," Reese denied quickly when Seever's scowl deepened. "No, Hector is definitely *not* my type."

Rubbing his palms over his shifter's chest—*my shifter,*

wow—Reese tried not to become too distracted by the feel of the smooth, tanned skin beneath his fingertips. For the first time in his life, Reese wasn't stopping himself from enjoying the feel of someone he was attracted to just because of his pre-conceived notion. He'd known others considered him prejudiced, and it was true, to a degree, but he'd always thought he had good reason.

Reese cleared his throat and held Seever's gaze. "I've always been attracted to people I didn't think I should want. So I stayed alone." He felt his cheeks heat, but he couldn't do anything about it. "When Rocky hooked up with Hector, at first, the changes in him confused and concerned me. Then I realized how happy he was. I . . . I wanted that. That happiness." Sighing deeply, Reese admitted, "I saw their devotion to each other. Hell, even Hector's love and care for Jayden, who isn't even his kid. I wanted to share in a bond like that."

"You wanted a mate," Seever murmured softly, his expression softening. He rubbed his hand over Reese's jaw, which caused the hairs on his nape to stand on end. "There's no shame in that, Reese. We all want someone to care about us and only us." Then his eyes narrowed, and his whiskey-brown eyes twinkled. "And now we have found each other, and after I claim you, we will live for centuries together, happily ever after."

"Happily ever after?" Reese repeated, amusement easing his embarrassment. The knowledge that Seever had accepted him so easily warmed him from the inside out. "How can you tell?" Then another tidbit snagged his attention. "Centuries?"

Seever nodded as he turned Reese and urged him to start walking again. As they fell into step together, with Reese tucked up against Seever's side, the larger man told him, "I'm a little over three hundred years old, Reese."

"Wow!"

Laughing, Seever waggled his brows as he grinned at him. "Hope you like older men."

Enjoying the shifter's playfulness, Reese hummed as he swept his gaze up and down Seever's body, appreciating the view. "I suppose you look all right for a guy your age."

Seever laughed, his happiness showing in the creases that lined his face when he did so. "Well, if I live to be around five hundred or so, which is average, that means we just might have two hundred years to spend together."

Reese allowed his right hand, which he'd placed on Seever's opposite hip when he'd turned him, to slide down and cover the shifter's sweatpants-covered ass. "I suppose I can work with that." He squeezed the firm globe, enjoying the way the muscled cheek filled his palm.

Growling playfully, Seever nipped at Reese's ear before kissing his neck. He didn't try to move Reese's hand, however, so Reese kept it there as they entered a side door. Reese enjoyed feeling up Seever's ass as they made their way through the twisting hallways of the estate.

"So, uh," Reese began when they stopped at a door that was two down from the one he recognized he'd been in. "What goes on in, uh, in bonding?"

Maybe I should have asked that before.

A wash of nerves swept through Reese.

Should I rethink this?

Except, Reese knew that thinking too hard had been what had sent him running in a panic in the first place. He overthought things. It was something he just couldn't seem to help doing—weigh the pros and cons over and over and over again.

"Relax, my mate," Seever crooned into his ear.

Reese blinked and realized he'd missed when they'd entered the room. They stood in a front living suite similar to Rocky and Hector's—minus the toys—but it was done in

65

subtle hues of green, instead of blue and tan. The room was comfortably appointed with two reclining chairs, a small sofa, and a flat-screened TV hanging over a wood-burning fireplace.

The place was . . . really nice.

Seever eased around Reese so they faced each other. He slid his hand up his shoulder to his neck, then teased his thumb over his pulse point. With his other hand, Seever gripped his hip, sliding his fingertips under his shirt to touch his skin.

"So . . . you asked about bonding," Seever began, lust filling his voice, making the direction of his thoughts easy enough to follow. "It's simple, but you need to understand the repercussions."

With the way Seever petted his neck and side, Reese found his thoughts scattering. "O-Oh?"

Damn it. I need to focus.

Reese cleared his throat and took a step backward, lifting his hands when Seever attempted to keep him close. "Like I said." He kept his smile warm as he spoke, not liking the hurt look that flitted ever-so-briefly across the man's face. "Your touch is damn distracting." Reese pointed at the couch. "Please. Sit and explain. You said repercussions. What are you talking about?"

Even as Seever did as he'd ordered, Reese wondered what he was thinking. His brows were furrowed, and his expression had turned guarded. Maybe he was regretting his choice of words.

Settling on the sofa next to Seever, Reese placed his hand on the man's thigh. He found himself in the surprising situation of wanting to soothe him.

Huh. Never felt that before.

Still, Reese rubbed Seever's thigh, squeezing and massaging lightly.

Seever smiled at Reese, the lines on his face smoothing

out. "Repercussions did sound ominous," he mused, placing his hand over Reese's and squeezing in return. "Still." Seever cleared his throat. "When we bond, which is done during sex." Once again his expression turned heated. With his free hand, Seever reached out and touched the spot on his neck where it met the meat of his shoulder. "I'll give you a claiming bite here while I spill my seed in your body." A low growl entered his tone as he continued, "It will combine our life forces so your aging will slow, allowing you to live as long as I do."

Reese shivered as goose bumps broke out on his upper arms just from that simple touch. Swallowing hard, he whispered hoarsely, "Okay. So far doesn't sound so bad."

Seever hummed and tipped his head, studying him for a few heartbeats. Then he lowered his hand and cradled Reese's between both his own where it rested on his thigh. "Pros and cons." After clearing his throat, Seever began, "Uh, pros . . . obviously, you live longer, you'll become healthier, less susceptible to disease, stronger bones, maybe a bit better senses." Pinning Reese with a feral smile, he added, "And of course, amazing sex with a shifter who will never get enough of you."

Sucking in a harsh breath, Reese felt a wash of heated arousal course through his body. He wanted to shout *yes, please* and then climb the man like a ladder. Having never responded to anyone that way, Reese reined in his desires.

"S-So, cons?" Reese pressed.

"Yeah, those." Seever heaved a sigh, then brought Reese's hand to his lips and kissed the knuckles before returning them to his lap. "Cons. Well, you'll outlive most anyone you know who isn't bonded with a paranormal. Every few decades we'll have to reinvent our identity." Seever's eyes turned a little vacant as he thought, humming softly. "Then there's the fact that if you do somehow end up injured, you'll have to go to a specialized type of doctor, one who knows about our kind, that way you don't run the risk of exposing our secrets or being turned into a guinea pig to discover why you're different."

Seever grimaced, quickly adding, "The big one, I suppose is the fact that if I die, you will, too."

"Wow!"

Reese couldn't stop himself from blurting out the word. He gaped at Seever, who stared intently at him. While his expression appeared calm, the way he continued to massage Reese's hand gave away his concern.

Even hearing what could be considered cons laid out for him, a rush of anticipation filled Reese. He swept his gaze over Seever's broad torso, noticing the pebbled tan nubs. A glance down confirmed it. Seever was aroused just by sitting next to him.

Deciding he needed to remove the uncertainty from him, Reese commented, "You forgot one con." He watched Seever's eyebrows shoot up, so he rolled one shoulder and teased, "I'd be getting a jealous boyfriend who wants to control where I go and when."

Seever's eyes narrowed. "You're forgetting the flip side of that, Reese," he countered, leaning toward him. "You will get a partner who cares about your happiness and safety with every fiber of his being." Seever's smile turned hungry, possessive. "And if that means knowing where you go and when, well . . . that's just so I know where to find you should I feel the urge to fuck you."

Sucking in a harsh breath, Reese tried to concentrate on his blithe response while keeping his voice from breaking with his need. "I-I'll have you know that I run a clean kitchen, Seever Kerns." Reese lifted his nose and pretended to look down at the man, which wasn't easy considering he was shorter than him even when sitting. "There will be no defiling my pristine surfaces with such behavior."

Seever groaned even as he lunged at Reese. "Fuck, the ideas you're giving me," he rasped, as he wrapped his arms around Reese and practically tossed him over his shoulder as he stood. "I will teach you to enjoy my defiling."

Reese laughed, shocked to find pleasure at being in such a position, upside down over another man's shoulder as he was carried away. "No you most certainly will not," he responded primly — well, as primly as one could while being carried like a sack of potatoes.

"Mouth," Seever snapped, although his tone held amusement. "I'll teach you to counter me."

Then, to Reese's shock, Seever smacked his ass. He gasped, shocked not only at the feel of the sting but upon the fact that his dick twitched. When Seever did it a second time, to his other butt cheek, Reese bit his bottom lip to hold in his moan. Unfortunately, he could do nothing about the way the sensation sent a zing to his balls, which caused a bead of pre-cum to ooze from his dick.

Seever moaned loud and low. "Oh, fucking hell," he ground out. "I smell your pre-cum, my mate. You like that." As he finished speaking, Seever slapped his hand over Reese's ass again, giving him another couple of swats.

Unable to help himself, Reese groaned. His hips twitched, causing his dick to rub across Seever's chest. A fresh wash of tingles flooded his groin.

"Oh, gods above and below," Seever cried, gripping Reese's hip to still his movements. "So fucking sexy. Gonna make your ass glow with my marks, and you're gonna love it."

Reese did love that idea, yet, he groaned in dismay at the loss of stimulation. It was then he realized that they'd stopped moving, and he found his gaze drifting to the bed at his left . . . then he focused on something else. His soon-to-be lover's gorgeous globes called to him.

Reaching down with both hands, Reese gripped them both. He squeezed and massaged, relishing that the weighty mounds felt even better than when he'd been walking back to the estate. His shifter's muscles flexed beneath his palms as a low rumbling growl escaped the man, but that only encouraged Reese to continue to enjoy the feel of their firmness.

"Playing with fire there, Reese," Seever stated huskily.

Without warning, Seever tossed Reese onto the bed. Reese bounced once, then the bigger man was on him. Seever pushed him to the center of the bed and pulled his legs apart, all while crawling up to settle between his calves.

Seever began undressing him, slowly, starting with his left shoe and sock. Pausing to massage Reese's foot, he held his gaze. "If you don't want this, say so now, my mate." Seever pressed into his insole, tearing a groan of pleasure from Reese's throat. "Otherwise"—Seever moved his ministrations to Reese's other foot, once it was bare, offering it the same treatment—"I'm going to claim you and bind us. Are you ready for that?"

Reese struggled to gather enough brain cells to give the question the consideration it deserved.

Am I ready? We met just this morning.

Seever even stilled his hand and held his gaze, waiting.

Spotting the warmth gleaming from their depths, Reese realized that Seever was offering him everything he'd ever wanted . . . and it was on a silver platter, no less.

"I'd be a fool to turn you down, Seever," Reese whispered softly, then gulped as he held the other man's gaze. "But that doesn't mean I don't still have some fears. If I, um, if I panic again, you'll help talk me off the ledge, right?"

Releasing his foot, Seever rested one hand on each calf, then skimmed them upward. He paused at Reese's knees, using his thumbs to massage the inside of his kneecaps. His expression held warmth, kindness, and even understanding.

"You, Reese, my mate, are my everything. If you ever have fears, I pray you'll do me the honor of sharing them with me." Then his gaze heated as a feral grin curved his lips. "And if that means making your buns burn with the heat of my palm to get you to talk, I'm all for it."

Reese moaned. He shouldn't have been so turned on by that threat—no, that promise—but he was.

Holding Seever's gaze, Reese nodded once before murmuring, "I admit I might still panic, Seever. I get lost in my head sometimes, but I do want what you're offering." He watched Seever's eyes dilate and his nostrils flare and thought the man's hunger had never looked sexier on anyone. Wanting more, wanting everything, Reese spread his legs wider and purred, "Make me yours."

Chapter Nine

Seever wanted to roar with triumph.
My mate has agreed.

Not wanting to scare his human, he held in the urge.

Instead, Seever skimmed his fingernails up Reese's thighs until his hands were poised at his fly. He remembered the sight and smell of his mate when he was blowing him, and a shiver of anticipation flooded him. Seever wanted to experience that again more than his next breath.

Seever made quick work of his mate's fly, then pulled his jeans and underwear down and off. After tossing them over the side of his bed, he returned his focus to Reese. His breath caught in his chest upon finding that his human had taken the initiative to pull off his polo shirt and toss it aside.

"Oh, Reese." Seever groaned and pressed the heel of his palm to the base of his prick. "So sexy, my mate."

For a long moment, Seever just stared. He licked his lips with his desire to taste every inch of the man's smooth, mocha-colored skin. His fingers itched to touch and massage.

As Seever reached for Reese, his mate lifted his hand and wagged a finger at him. "Uh uh," he countered. Then he pointed at Seever's groin. "You're overdressed."

Groaning at his oversight, Seever slipped off the bed. He quickly shucked his sweatpants and kicked them off as he straightened. When he returned his focus back to the bed, he hummed in smug satisfaction.

"I like the way you're looking at me, Reese," Seever claimed. His mate was looking at him as if he were a steak and he wanted to gobble him up. "Hmmm." Seever reached down and gripped the base of his dick and gave himself a slow, leisurely stroke. He bit back a hiss at the pressure on his sensitive flesh. Instead, he smirked as he winked at Reese. "See something you like?"

Reese with a feral grin on his face was a damn fine-looking specimen of maleness. "Why don't you grab the lube, get up here, and I'll show you?"

More than on board with that idea, Seever let go of himself and grabbed the handle to the nightstand's top drawer. He pulled it open and snagged the needed slick. When he returned his focus to his bed, he nearly swallowed his tongue.

Reese had gotten onto his knees, resting his weight on his calves. His legs were splayed, and he jacked his long, slender, deep-brown rod with his right hand. With his left fingers, Reese teased at one distended dark bud.

His back was arched as he moved into his hands. He had his head thrown back, and his lips were parted. Nibbling on his bottom lip, he showed off white teeth as he clearly enjoyed himself.

"Oh, babe." Seever groaned deep in his throat. He gripped his balls and tugged, easing his sudden need to come. "So damn pretty."

Giving Seever a lazy smile, Reese lifted his hand from his nipple and slipped his forefingers into his mouth. He sucked on them for a few seconds as he stared at Seever with a heavy-lidded gaze. After pulling his fingers free with a lewd pop, he rose up on his knees, stuck out his ass, and reached behind himself. A second later, Reese let out a long, low moan that practically vibrated Seever's balls.

"Fuck," Seever whined. "I wanna see."

"Get on the bed," Reese ordered, panting. "On your back."

Seever scrambled to obey. As soon as his back hit the comforter, Reese was moving. He watched with anticipation as his mate swung his leg over his torso, pointing his butt in his direction, putting everything on display. Reese's forefingers were still buried in his hole, stretching the muscles. His balls dangled between his legs, round and swollen. Every few heartbeats, Seever received a view of Reese's slender, bouncing cock as it twitched, then dipped, only to bounce back up toward his stomach.

"Reese," Seever murmured, his voice low and dripping with his appreciation. "So pretty."

Needing to participate, Seever snapped the cap off the lube and poured a healthy dollop onto his fingers. He reached up and spread it over Reese's striated muscle. A second later, he pushed his slick finger in beside his lover's pair.

Hot, tight pressure clamped down on his digit at the same time as a sweet, low keening sound filled the air.

My mate makes beautiful music.

"My sweet mate," Seever rumbled around a moan of his own. "So gorgeous. So responsive. And all mine."

"Seever," Reese cried. "Another one. Please!"

"Sure, babe." Seever leaned to the side and nipped at the inside of Reese's thigh. At the same time, he edged a second finger into his lover. "Yeah. Take it."

Between them both, they had four fingers inside his man's tunnel. The striated ring of muscle was stretched so nicely, causing the normally dark skin to whiten at the edges. He used a slippery thumb to massage that flesh, hoping to ease discomfort. At the same time, Seever crooked his fingers, searching for that intimate, pleasure-giving nub.

When Reese barked a cry and jolted above him, Seever knew he'd found it. He spotted his human's shaft bobbing between his legs. Wanting to feel that smooth skin, too, he reached for it and wrapped his fingers around it.

"Seever!"

Seever began slowly jacking his mate as he worked his fingers in and out of his ass. Noting that Reese's fingers were frozen, he grinned widely. He'd completely immobilized his sexy mate.

Seever's smug satisfaction soared.

A second later, Seever let out a gasp of his own. Hot, wet suction surrounded his shaft. A thick appendage tickled the sensitive wrinkled flesh beneath his crown, only to swipe over his glans over and over. Then Reese went deep, swallowing him to the root.

Bellowing his pleasure, Seever shuddered beneath his mate's sweet tongue. When Reese pulled his fingers out of his chute to bring his arm around, maybe for balance, Seever instantly replaced them with one of his own thicker digits. That caused Reese to moan deeply, sending delicious vibrations up Seever's erection. It nearly did him in when Reese's gentle fingers began to slide over and around his testicles, fondling them lightly.

That explained the need for his other hand for balance.

The thought was there and gone as a tingle started at the base of his spine. His balls began to tighten. Clenching his abdominals, he groaned with his attempt to control himself.

To Seever's relief, just then Reese popped off his dick.

"Please, Seever," Reese whined, wiggling his hips, pulling partly away. "Please fuck me."

"Thought you'd never ask," Seever snarled. He eased his fingers free and released Reese's dick. Hearing his mate moan, Seever smacked Reese's very fine ass, admiring the redness that immediately erupted—not to mention the soft inhalation of pleasure from his mate—as he ordered, "Crawl forward."

As Reese obeyed, Seever poured more slick onto his fingers. Bending his knees, he quickly rolled and climbed onto them. As he knee-walked into position behind Reese's upturned ass, Seever lubed up his dick, then gripped the base, barely stemming his growing need to erupt.

Seever feared he would blow as soon as he sank into his mate. Gripping his balls with his other hand, he squeezed and twisted. He gritted his teeth as his need for release eased.

Taking a deep breath, Seever moved his clean hand to Reese's flank. He dipped his head and nuzzled at his lover's warm ass cheek while pushing his fingers once again into Reese's hole, enjoying the view of how the muscles stretched. At the same time, Seever slid his hand up his mate's side and fondled the lines of his ribs.

"P-Please, Seever. Please."

"Yessss, my mate," Seever hissed, his heartrate spiking upon hearing his sexy human beg. While pulling his fingers free and slotting up behind him, he rumbled, "Now I make you mine."

"Yes!"

Seever took Reese's cried word as the best kind of acceptance. Pushing against his lover's well-prepared hole, his crown easily sank into his mate. The muscles of Reese's chute immediately clamped onto him, yanking a groan from his throat.

Draping over Reese's smaller body, Seever nuzzled Reese's nape with his lips. He rested his weight on his right hand so he could continue fondling his lover's chest. Finding his human's nipple, he squeezed lightly.

Reese trembled beneath him even as he let out a long sigh. His chute relaxed, relinquishing its death grip on Seever's cock head. As Seever began easing deeper into his mate, then withdrawing, then deeper again, Reese let out a string of moans and whimpers, groans and mewls.

Every sweet noise was music to Seever's ears. He loved how vocal, how uninhibited his human was. He hoped to draw so many more wonderful noises from him with each new exploration.

Right at that moment though, as he stopped his strokes with his erection buried balls deep, Seever's instincts were riding him hard. His need to claim, to make Reese his own, to see his human carrying his mark, roared through him like a freight train. He trembled as the last vestiges of his control began to unravel.

"Y-You ready?" Seever asked.

If his mate asked for a minute, Seever didn't know how he would manage it.

Reese growled as he glared over his shoulder at Seever. "If you don't move right now, I'm gonna buck you off and ride you like a pogo stick."

Seever bit back a laugh. Instead, he reared up, moving his right hand to Reese's hip and gripping tightly. He used his left hand to smack the side of his mate's ass.

His mate moaned and trembled in his grasp. His chute muscles clenched and released, offering a sensuous massage. He even mewled oh-so-pleasantly.

Loving that response, Seever did it again, but then his control was shot.

Seever gripped both of Reese's hips in a tight hold and eased out until his dick's crown tugged at his mate's entrance. He reversed directions. Seeing his erection disappearing into Reese's body, a primal burst of pleasure surged through him.

"Mine," Seever snarled as he picked up his pace.

His cat urged Seever on, and he felt his gums tingle, his canines threatening to drop. Parting his lips, panting harshly, he didn't fight it when they descended. Seever's mouth watered as his focus riveted to Reese's pulse point.

Seever had just enough presence of mind to adjust his angle. On his second try, he felt the ripple of pleasure that went through Reese's body. His mate bucked in his hold as he let out a bark of ecstasy.

"Yesss," Seever hissed, his words slightly slurred around his longer teeth. "Cry out for me," he demanded. "Share your pleasure."

"S-Seever! Oh, yes. Fuck, right there. There. There. Seever!"

Reese howled and twitched in Seever's hold. His chute muscles rippled along his length. Even his back arched as if to better present himself.

The repeated clenching along Seever's overly sensitized length felt as if Reese was trying to suck his orgasm from him. The base of his spine tingled, and his balls pulled flush. His release pulsed through Seever in blissful waves.

Seever roared his joy at marking his mate's insides. Then his gaze lowered to Reese's neck, to the succulent flesh at the curve. His mouth watered, and he gave in to the instinct to taste, to bite and mark.

Lowering over his lover's sweat-slicked torso, Seever licked a stripe up the side of his neck. His cat howled in triumph when Reese tilted his head, offering more room. Taking that as an invitation, Seever struck.

Blood oozed around his canines as he sank them into Reese's flesh. He swiped his tongue around his teeth while sealing his lips over the wound. The iron-rich flavor of his mate's life-blood burst across his taste buds, making them sing, and his senses reeled.

Moaning against Reese's flesh, Seever sucked for more.

Our bond is complete.

Greater satisfaction than Seever had ever felt before hit him when Reese cried out and trembled in his arms. He scented the enticing fragrance of his mate's cum flood the air anew. The knowledge that his bite had caused Reese to orgasm again was almost better than the knowledge that he'd completed their bond.

Almost.

Nothing was better than pleasing his mate.

Humming happily, Seever carefully eased his teeth free of Reese's neck. He licked at the wounds, closing the tooth marks and lapping up the last of Reese's amazing blood. Peering down at his mark on Reese's neck, Seever hummed happily.

"So fucking sexy, so perfect." Seever kissed the mark, then whispered, "And so very mine."

Reese moaned, then broke into a soft chuckle. "H-Holy shit, Seeve," he mumbled. "That shouldn't have been possible."

"What?" Even though his prick had softened to half-mast, Seever didn't want to pull out, yet, to lose that connection. Instead, he wrapped one arm tightly around Reese's chest, then eased them to their right sides. While Reese grunted softly, he didn't respond, so Seever pressed, "What shouldn't be possible?"

Spotting the enticing curve of Reese's dark-bronze-skinned neck, Seever leaned forward to kiss and nibble at the tempting flesh.

"Three orgasms in less than a couple of hours," Reese answered, his voice muffled and his tone groggy. A second later, he snorted. "Anything I've seen and heard today."

Damn. Have I really known my mate for less than a day?

Heaving a soft sigh, Seever rubbed his left hand lightly along the lines of Reese's smooth, lean torso. "I'm sure the paranormal world takes some getting used to, but you'll get there, Reese." He nuzzled his cheek against the back of his human's neck, enjoying the short, slightly rough hair there. "I have faith in you."

Reese hummed. "So, according to the movies, now that we're enjoying post-coital relaxation, this is where we're supposed to share our histories with each other." Turning his head, he met Seever's gaze. "Is that something a paranormal would do, too?"

"Hmmm," Seever hummed. "Certain history, sure."

Wincing, he admitted, "I have no desire to hear about your past sexual exploits, but everything else . . . absolutely."

Scoffing, Reese admitted, "I don't want to hear about your past sex life, either, Seever." He turned his head enough to meet his gaze over his shoulder. "I mean, you said you were over three hundred years old, so you must have been with, like, at least that many over the years."

Seever grinned, trying to make light of their line of conversation. "Let's just say, those people were a long line of nameless, faceless people, and you are the only one for me from now on." Recalling something he hadn't mentioned, he admitted, "Hell, as a bonded shifter, I can't even get it up for anyone but you."

Reese lifted on his arm and turned. The movement pulled Seever's softened cock from his human's channel, drawing hisses from them both. Then Reese pressed against him so he could meet his gaze more fully.

"Are you serious?"

"I am," Seever assured. Sliding his clean hand along his mate's neck, he teased the pads of his forefingers over his claiming mark. "You're it for me."

"Damn. That kinda takes monogamy to a whole new level, doesn't it?" The corners of Reese's lips kicked up around the edges. "Does it make me an asshole that I really like that news?"

Seever chuckled as he shook his head. "Not at all."

Reese hummed softly, cuddling against him. Then he winced.

"What's wrong?" Seever rubbed his chest, concerned.

"Um, never fucked bare. It's . . . unusual." Reese's cheeks took on a darker hue as he asked, "Can we clean up?"

Dismissing the image of Reese with others—no sense pissing off his cat—Seever immediately nodded. "Absolutely. Let's go soak in the jetted tub and clean up, then we'll nap. Hmm?"

"Jetted tub?" Reese grinned broadly. "Nice!" As his human allowed Seever to pull him to his feet, he asked, "Will you share other tidbits about shifter life with me? Like what the council does and why that Cabo guy attacked your boss? How long have you been working for him?"

Seever chuckled, loving the fact that his mate suddenly had so many questions. "Absolutely," he replied, pecking a kiss to his lips. "Bath with relaxing salts and question and answer time. Let's go."

Then Seever led the way into his spacious bathroom ensuite and the promised jetted tub.

Chapter Ten

"So, how long do you think it will be until your parents visit?"

Glancing over at Rocky, who leaned against the far kitchen counter, Reese grimaced. As he kneaded the bread dough, he thought about the conversation with his mom and dad which he'd had two nights before. "Not long," he warned. "They were seriously pissed that I didn't come back at all."

"Well, you're the one who commissioned a moving company to pack up your apartment and move you without a word to them." Rocky grinned broadly, clearly amused by Reese's predicament. "You could have accepted our help. A few of us would have gone back and done it with you."

Shaking his head, Reese placed the dough in a bowl, then covered it with a clean cloth. It would need some time to rise before he could bake it. He anticipated the look of pleasure on Seever's face when he realized there was fresh bread. His mate loved it, especially if it was warm and right out of the oven.

Over the last nearly two weeks together, Reese had become damn good at anticipating Seever's schedule. He loved timing it just right to offer some kind of treat to his man first thing. Well, after they'd shared a hello kiss, of course.

Seever's schedule often kept him busy in the afternoon. The problems created by a couple of ex-councilmen kept him on his toes. Evidently, they kept moving around, and even though they'd received information from captured assholes, they still hadn't caught up with them.

Reese hoped they would soon. His poor man was running himself ragged.

"Earth to Reese. Come in, Reese."

Rocky's deep voice sing-songing words snapped Reese out of his thoughts. Turning away from the empty counter, he frowned at his cousin. "What?"

"I was asking what the real reason was that you didn't take the flock up on our offer to move you."

Reese had become pretty good friends with most of the people Rocky called his flock-mates. Especially Thad, since he occasionally shared the kitchen with him. He hadn't been too surprised to find out the shorter, thickly muscled man turned into a wild turkey. What had shocked him, however, was the fact that Thad found cooking relaxing.

Oddly enough, Reese found he liked the brusque man.

"Reese?"

Recalling Rocky's question, Reese headed to the sink to wash his hands. Over his shoulder, he told him, "The long and the short of it? Seever couldn't get away, and I didn't want to leave him." He shrugged one shoulder as he added a bit more soap, so he could work off all the bits of dough and flour embedded into the creases of his fingers. "Our bond is too new."

Rocky's large warm hand came down on his shoulder and squeezed gently. His cousin's huge form appeared in Reese's peripheral, so he looked that way. He was surprised to see Rocky smiling warmly at him.

"Now *that* I understand perfectly, cuz." Rocky grinned once more. "So, did you tell Seever that your birthday is next week?"

"He knows." Reese scowled at his cousin, unhappy with the gleam he spotted in his dark eyes. "And I told him I'm not a fan of parties."

Heaving a sigh, Rocky furrowed his brows. "Did you at least tell him why?" he mumbled, crossing his arms over his chest as he stared at the floor.

Reese hated thinking about his youthful stupidity. Back when he was fourteen, he'd thought he was making friends with the rich, popular crowd in his class at the public school he'd attended. He'd been invited to one of the kids' birthday parties.

As it had turned out, as soon as Reese had arrived, they'd started harassing him . . . about everything. They'd picked on his clothes, smacked him around a bit, and made fun of his family, calling them poor niggers, as well as a few other nasty slurs. Reese had fled, and those same assholes had found discreet ways to make fun of him for the rest of their time in school together.

Reese shut off the water and grabbed a couple of paper towels, then he began drying his hands. Turning back to face Rocky, he nodded.

"Yeah. I told him."

Rocky grinned at that. "Good. When will those lemon bars be finished?" Just that fast, his cousin accepted and moved on. "Hector is looking forward to 'em."

Chuckling softly, Reese glanced at the white dial counter sitting on the countertop. "That one is for the lemon bars, so . . . ten minutes."

"Then what's that timer for?" Rocky pointed at the countdown happening on the bottom oven's display.

That one read forty-seven minutes.

"The pot roast's baking in there." Reese's mouth watered just thinking about it. "I need to check the water level and add the vegetables when that finishes counting down, then I'll reset it."

Rocky hummed, his eyebrows furrowing. "So, why don't you use the timer on the top oven?"

Reese knew why his cousin asked. That was where the lemon bars were baking, after all. Reese loved the kitchen's double oven.

Chuckling, Reese explained, "The timer button on that one is broken. Got pressed one too many times, I guess." He shrugged. "I keep meaning to tell Seever, but he has so much else on his plate that—"

Rocky lifted his hands. "Say no more. I—"

Reese felt his phone vibrate in his pocket. "Oh, hold up." As he pulled the phone from his pants, he watched Rocky cross to the left refrigerator and pulled out a bottle of iced tea. Glancing at the screen, Reese felt a measure of surprise fill him, and he pushed the accept button. "Hey, Seever. What's up?"

His lover was in a meeting in the front room. He was one of three enforcers who were there to watch the councilman's back as he met with Alpha Sturgis Marsden, the leader of Cabo's cougar pride. The way Reese understood it, he was there with Cabo's sister, Alba, as well as a couple of his own enforcers.

While Reese didn't understand the posturing, Seever had assured him that it was normal.

"Hi, babe," Seever rumbled into the phone.

Even from those two words, Reese could read the tension. Somehow, a meeting that was only supposed to last fifteen minutes and was going over thirty, was not going well.

"Will you bring more beverages, please? And a selection of those meat and fruit pastries you made yesterday?"

"Of course. I'll load a cart and bring it in as soon as possible," Reese assured, concern riding him. He wanted to ask so many questions but stayed his tongue. Now wasn't the time.

Later.

"Thank you, my mate," Seever continued, a hint of relief in his tone. "I'll have Beakner escort you."

Huh.

"Okay."

Reese left it at that, and Seever disconnected the call.

Hearing Rocky clear his throat, he turned to find his cousin close—probably close enough to hear the conversation—and lifted both brows in silent question. Then he went to the massive pantry and pulled out a rolling cart with three tiers.

"So, food and drink for a meeting going long," Rocky mused slowly in his deep rumbling voice.

Placing the cart near the refrigerator, Reese saw that his cousin was already pulling out the trays of pastries he'd baked the prior evening. The first thing Reese had learned while cooking for the people of the estate was that shifters had huge appetites. Every recipe he knew, he'd had to get used to quadrupling.

It meant some adjustments, but Reese truly enjoyed it. At the estate, he was the master of his domain. Of course, the owner of *Southwestern Bar & Grill*, Mister Lagrange, had just about gone off the rails when Reese had quit with no notice. Reese had felt a bit bad, leaving the restaurant in the lurch that way . . . but that sensation had fled pretty quickly when Lagrange had proceeded to cuss him out, then vow that Reese would never work in the food industry again.

Seever had entered the front room of their suite where Reese had been making the call. The shifter had been in the bedroom folding laundry and had somehow sensed Reese's distress. He'd gently taken the phone from Reese's hand, had lifted it to his own face and ordered, "Don't call this number again," then disconnected the line. He'd turned off the phone and tossed it onto the sofa before leading Reese to the bedroom.

The loving that afternoon had been slow and sweet, and the memory of it still caused Reese's dick to thicken.

Of course, with Seever around, that was a common occurrence, too.

Reese couldn't remember ever having so much sex.

"Earth to Reese. Come in, Reese."

Once again, Rocky's sing-songed words cut into Reese's thoughts.

Barking a laugh, Reese shoved his elbow into the bigger man's upper arm. Rocky laughed as he rocked away from him. Grinning, Reese began placing plates of different trays onto the cart.

Reese and Rocky had been close when younger, almost like they were true brothers. As the years had passed and their lives had gone in different directions, however, they'd drifted apart. Then Rocky had found Hector, and they'd rarely spent any time together.

After bonding with Seever, Reese finally understood. It had been his own insecurities and prejudices that had caused the rift. Reese had thought he was protecting himself, when in reality, he'd been isolating himself.

Life at the estate had changed everything . . . and so had his time with Seever.

"What do you think's going on?" Reese asked as he continued to fill the cart. "What could have caused a need for refreshments?"

Rocky shrugged. "Maybe the alpha sprang information on the councilman that they hadn't known or anticipated, making an even bigger mess." Pouring a fresh pot of coffee into a carafe, he flashed a grin in Reese's direction. "Maybe they found common ground and want to be friends."

Reese snorted as he did something similar with a pot of decaf coffee. "How come I think it's probably closer to option A?"

"Because you're a smart man, Reese," his cousin replied.

Scoffing, Reese pointed at the timers. "Can you stick around and pull out the lemon bars?" An uneasy niggle in the back of his mind told him he wasn't going to make it back to the kitchen in . . . seven minutes.

"Will do," Rocky agreed with a wink. "Wouldn't want to

disappoint Hector."

Reese chuckled as he nodded, even as he added a glass container holding an assortment of tea bags on the cart. Finally, he added a carafe of hot water and a small bowl of lemon slices. Rocky handed him the bottle of honey, which he also added while murmuring his thanks.

"Ready, Reese?" Beakner asked, announcing his presence as he opened the double doors at the front end of the kitchen. They led to the formal dining room, and there was plenty of room to maneuver the cart.

Nodding, Reese began pushing the cart toward the doors. He was used to Beakner's minimalistic communication skills. Somewhere along the line, Reese had learned that Beakner had spent several decades living in his alligator form until a housing development had driven his animal from his home.

Reese joined Beakner, and the pair made their way to the front of the house. The hairs on the back of his neck stood up the closer they drew to the salon. Beakner paused in front of the doors, lifting his hand for him to stop.

After Reese had obeyed, Beakner drew close to him. He peered at him intently with his deep brown eyes. "Take a couple of slow, deep breaths, Reese," he murmured softly. "You don't want to go in there smelling of anxiety."

"Shit, right."

Shifters and their damn uber-sensitive noses.

Reese took a slow deep breath, then a second one. After the third one, he felt a little calmer. He reminded himself that Seever was behind that door, and there was no way his lover would put him in any danger.

"There ya go," Beakner mumbled, nodding. "The alpha and his people are seated on the right, toward the front of the house, so you immediately maneuver to the left. There's plenty of space behind the sofa that Seever and Vincentius are sitting on. They will guide you once you're in position."

Great. Rules for meeting with strangers.

Even though Reese wished he could leave the tray with Beakner and go back to the safety of his kitchen, he nodded his understanding instead. Seever had asked for him. He couldn't deny his lover.

Beakner knocked twice, then opened the door without waiting for a response. He stepped to the right, effectively forcing Reese to head left. That was okay, since there wasn't much room toward the front windows anyway.

The sofa was occupied by a large, imposing-looking, dirty-blond haired man. Next to him sat a woman with thick blonde hair done in an elegant plait that disappeared behind her. Behind them stood three men, all with various shades of blond hair. All five of the people were good-looking.

Not as fine as my man.

As Reese pushed the cart to the left and around the sofa, he caught Seever's eye. His shifter smiled at him, then beckoned. "Leave that, babe," he urged. "Come sit with me."

More than happy to do that, Reese relinquished control to dishing out the refreshments to Lachlan. The wildcat shifter gave him a slight chin nod in acknowledgement, then he took over pushing the cart. Thad stayed close by, and an enforcer named Johnnie stood near Vincentius.

While crossing to Seever's side, Reese heard the woman snort. He ignored her in favor of taking his mate's hand. His lover immediately urged him down, fitting him into the small space between Seever and the arm of the large sofa.

Good thing he was slender.

"Thanks for coming, babe," Seever murmured, wrapping his arm around his shoulders. "It seems this pair has a question about what a true mate-bond is."

"Really?" Reese cocked his head as he eyed the pair across from them. The dozen feet, divided by a coffee table, put them a little too close for comfort. Still, Reese was a little curious. "I thought shifters knew about matings since birth."

Then he snorted softly. "Or puberty anyway when their parents explain the birds and the bees to 'em."

Seever nodded as he accepted a cup of coffee from Thad. "That is supposed to be true, yes." Then his attention turned to the couple on the sofa. "However, there are those that refuse to accept that Fate does give us our mates in humans and those of the same sex."

"If Fate did that, we would die out," the man Reese pegged as Alpha Sturgis Marsden stated. His ice-blue eyes narrowed as he glanced between them. "So this is a choice you've made, not fated mates."

Reese couldn't help it. He laughed.

"Why does the human laugh?" Sturgis demanded.

"Probably found your statement funny," Councilman Vincentius stated just as the door opened. "Ah, Cho, my love." He patted his lap. "Please sit with me."

Pressing his palm to his stomach, Reese bent a little as he tried to catch his breath. He grinned, slowly catching his breath. Focusing on Sturgis, Reese caught the man's eye.

Even the annoyed gleam in the cat shifter's eye couldn't keep Reese from speaking his mind. "It's so damn obvious that you haven't met your true mate, yet." Reese saw Sturgis's eyes narrow and felt Seever tighten his hold on him. Still, he plunged ahead. "Hell, I'm human, knew nothing about paranormals, and I still couldn't resist the draw of my shifter for more than a few hours." Reaching up, Reese pulled the collar of his polo shirt away from his neck, showing off his neck and Seever's claiming mark there. "Allowing my mate to claim me was the most amazing experience of my life." He grinned broadly and waggled his brows. "If you get the chance to experience it, you will *totally* be eating your words."

Chapter Eleven

Seever just managed to bite back his laugh. His mate was so right. Since Alpha Sturgis hadn't met his mate or felt the mind-scrambling pull provided by Fate, he truly just couldn't understand.

Alpha Sturgis's low growl filled the room. At the same time, Alba — Cabo's sister and the pride's current alpha-mate — sneered as she stated, "How dare you speak to the alpha in such a manner, *human*." She spoke the word as if it were something dirty. "You're nothing but a lower life form. Good only for service." Alba's eyes narrowed as she curled her lips in disgust. "Or food for a vampire. *Cattle*."

"Wow, you're a bitch," Reese responded calmly. Then he turned toward Thad. "Hey, will you give me a cheese and strawberry-filled pastry. They're on the bottom right."

Leaping to her feet, Alba opened her mouth, her face turning red with her rage.

Seever tensed, readying himself just in case she decided to be a moron and start an inter-pack incident by attacking.

Sorta like her brother did. This is a family of hotheads.

Before Alba could speak, Alpha Sturgis grabbed her near arm and yanked her back into her seat. Seever found himself impressed despite himself at the big male's show of strength. Alba huffed, turning to glare at him.

Except, Alpha Marsden was hardly sparing her a glance. His focus was riveted on the shifter guard who'd escorted Cho to the room — Cassidy. A glance toward Cassidy revealed the guard sported a shell-shocked expression.

Well, damn. This just became awkward.

"What is your problem?" Alba demanded, obviously unused to being ignored by her mate. "Sturgis?" It wasn't until she smacked the back of her hand on the alpha's thigh that he yanked his attention away from Cassidy and focused on her glaring visage. "Are you seriously going to let that little *cretin* speak to you like that?"

"The human was right," Alpha Sturgis replied, his voice soft and low. He glanced toward Cassidy again, then focused on Reese. "My apologies, Seever's mate. I did not understand . . . until now."

Alba's eyes narrowed, their blue depths gleaming with maliciousness. "Surely you did not just agree with him. With that faggot. That worthless excuse for space. He just said that—"

"I heard what he said," the alpha cut in, barely raising his voice. The iciness of the man's tone was enough to chill just about the stiffest spine. His enforcers straightened, their surprise evident. "And like I said. He's right. We cannot judge others in regards to something we have never before experienced." Narrowing his pale blue eyes, the cougar alpha rumbled, "It is the height of hubris. And in my pride, it ends here."

Peering over his shoulder at the man in the middle, Alpha Sturgis met the other man's light brown eyes. "Beta Rufus Phoenin?"

"Yes, Alpha?"

Alpha Marsden rose, half-turning so he faced Alba while keeping the sofa where Seever and their people sat in his periphery. The beta was to his right. The alpha peered down at Alba, who was feigning an innocent look.

Yeah. That's not working so well for her at this point.

"Alba Limman, in the presence of my beta and enforcers, as well as Councilman Goldstein of the Shifter Council, I hereby dissolve our mate-bond." Alpha Sturgis's voice remained steady, keeping his words slow and clear. "No longer do you carry the title of alpha-mate, and you will remove all possessions from the pride lodge, returning to the dwelling of your ancestors, where you before resided with your brother, Cabo." His focus remained steady on Alba, even as she stared wide-eyed and clearly disbelieving right back at him. "Do you understand what has happened here, Alba Limman?"

Seever couldn't help but notice that during the course of Alpha Sturgis's decree, Alba's cheeks had grown darker and darker. The scent of her rising rage permeated the room. Her jaw was clenched so tightly, Seever could see a tick pulsing at her cheek.

"Alba Limman." Beta Rufus touched Alba's shoulder. "Answer the alpha."

Alba exploded into action. Leaping to her feet, she lunged at Vincentius and Cho, already shifting, her body expanding and tearing out of her clothes. The councilman responded by pushing Cho at Cassidy, but it was Beakner who grabbed the councilman's mate and yanked him clear of danger.

Even as Seever, too, shifted, he noticed Reese flip over the arm of the sofa and roll off to the side. Johnnie grabbed the back of the couch and yanked, causing it to tumble backward. Vincentius fluidly did a backward roll, getting out of the way.

Alba hit Johnnie, who was still in human form. The iron-rich smell of blood bloomed in the air coupled with the guard's pained cry.

Seever slammed into the female cougar. Sinking his claws into her shoulders, he batted her away from Johnnie. Unfortunately, that sent her rolling in the direction of the doorway where Cho still stood with Beakner. She tucked her legs under her and leaped toward the pair.

Cassidy slammed the door shut, offering an obstruction. Then he executed a dive-forward roll to the right, ducking under the attacking cougar. She slammed her head and shoulder into the fortified door, but Seever still heard a crack.

Another hit like that and she might break through.

Just as Seever pounced on her back, a cougar bigger than he'd ever seen before landed on his back. Twisting and swiping, he connected with Alba's shoulder and pushed away from the pair. Instead of following Seever, the cougar latched onto Alba's neck and forced her submission.

"If you could please *not* kill her, I would very much like the opportunity to question her."

Upon hearing Vincentius's dryly spoken request, Seever moved to stand in front of him. He felt the councilman touch his shoulder and offered a low rumbling roar back. Then, unable to help himself, Seever quickly glanced around the room.

Relief flooded him when he spotted Reese standing behind Thad. Lachlan, however, was crouched over Johnnie, using his own shirt to attempt to stem the bleeding from the wound on his torso. Johnnie appeared pale, and his eyes were glassy, but at least they were open.

Damn it all!

Seever returned his attention to the pair of cougars just in time to watch the big male ease his grip from Alba's neck. Immediately, another big cougar crouched close to her. Seever realized it was Beta Rufus, since both enforcers were still in human form. He was obviously on watch to keep her from resuming her attack. Seever wouldn't put it past her, since her brother had submitted then run once free.

Like brother, like sister.

When the big alpha shifted, Vincentius smirked at him. "I think you're the biggest cougar I've ever seen," he stated mildly. "And I asked Cho to join us to prove that mates come in different species, not so one of yours can attack him." A growl filled his voice. "*Again.*"

Alpha Sturgis dipped his head in a brief nod of respect and acknowledgement. "My apologies for what members of my pride have brought to your door." Then he met Vincentius's gaze squarely. "Will you give me Ezekiel's new address so I may approach him with the offer of restitution?"

"If your offer is sincere," Vincentius replied. "However, let's get Alba out of here first." He snapped his fingers and pointed at her. "If your beta is amenable to helping Beakner take your ex-alpha-mate downstairs."

His comment drew a snarl from the female cougar, and Vincentius smirked at her.

"Of course." With a look, Alpha Sturgis gave the order to the beta, who immediately nodded. "And may I trouble you for some sweatpants?"

"I'll get you a pair. For Seever, too," Cassidy mumbled from where he stood near the door, then he opened it and slipped out.

The gap was immediately replaced by the head of a massive alligator, which Seever recognized as Beakner in animal form.

Between the big cougar beta and the alligator, they herded Alba out of the room. Once she was gone, Cho rushed into the room and slammed into Vincentius's body. The councilman wrapped his small mate in his arms, hugging him close.

For several long seconds, Alpha Sturgis gazed after those who'd disappeared, then he cleared his throat and rounded the sofa he'd been sitting on. He grabbed a throw pillow and rested it on the back, effectively hiding his groin.

"I'll find Arlon," Thad stated.

Seever knew that with the departure of Doctor Cooper, Arlon was the best they had. He'd been trained in triage while in the military, but he hadn't pursued it after *dying* in World War II, so he could remake his identity. Still, some help was better than nothing.

"Thanks, my mate," Lachlan murmured where he was still trying to stem the flow of blood.

Thad nodded, then strode swiftly from the room.

Reese had moved to his side, doing his best to help, although he looked a little pale.

Seever didn't know if it was the sight of all the blood on Johnnie's body, or if it was from having to watch them shift and fight.

I'll ask later.

"So, is there anything you wish to share, Alpha Sturgis?" Councilman Vincentius asked, his tone containing a hint of teasing. "Maybe the reason you so swiftly changed your mind?" He began moving toward his downed guard even as he kept glancing at the alpha. All the while, he kept Cho tucked close against him. Without waiting for an answer from the alpha, Vincentius crouched beside Johnnie. "How is he doing?"

"I-I'll be okay," Johnnie ground out roughly.

"Sure you will," Lachlan agreed, his expression kinder than Seever had ever seen him look at anyone outside his mate. "A day or two and you'll be back on your feet."

"Here, Mister Kerns," Cassidy murmured, holding a pair of sweatpants in his line of sight.

Taking them in his mouth, Seever padded to the other side of the room, set them down, then proceeded to shift. After only a few seconds, he rose to his feet and pulled on the sweatpants. Seever immediately crossed to Reese and knelt beside him.

"Are you okay?" Seever asked softly, resting his palm on his mate's back. He rubbed up and down his spine soothingly. Being able to touch his mate helped calm his own pulse.

Reese flashed a tight smile his way even as he nodded. "I should be asking you that." He glanced pointedly at the long scrape down Seever's arm. "You're the one who was just in a fight."

Seever peered at his wound. "Huh. Didn't notice that."

Leaning over, he pecked a kiss to Reese's lips. "I love that you worry about me. Hope that doesn't make me too big an asshole."

To Seever's relief, Reese's tension eased from his body. He bumped Seever's shoulder with his upper arm, then murmured, "Only a little, but I don't mind."

Arlon arrived with his older brother, Jessup, as well as their vampire friend, Bashir. The shifter swiftly took over, and the trio carried Johnnie out of the room. A few seconds later, Beta Rufus and Guard Beakner returned. Both men already wore sweatpants, most likely provided by Beakner, since stashes of the item were throughout the house.

In a shifter home, that was just a normal precaution.

Finally, Alpha Sturgis answered the councilman's earlier question. "I realized your human mate was correct, Enforcer Seever, because" — he turned his attention on Cassidy — "you are my mate." The alpha had resumed his seat, but on the other side of the sofa — where Alba had been sitting — and he patted the cushion beside him. "Will you sit with me? Tell me your name?"

Not at all surprised, Seever wondered how the normally outgoing shifter would respond. He couldn't remember the last time he'd seen the man so reserved.

Cassidy sighed deeply from where he leaned against the wall. He thrust his hand through his hair, clearly hesitating, then he shook his head. He held up both hands, palms out in placation.

"I think you need to wrap this issue up with Councilman Vincentius first, Alpha," Cassidy responded quickly. "Better deal with one problem at a time. Ya know?"

Alpha Sturgis probably wouldn't have sported a different expression if someone had slapped him. "You believe being mated with me is . . . is a problem?"

Cassidy grimaced, then pointed one finger at the enforcer

behind the alpha.

Seever watched as Alpha Sturgis turned his head. From his own position across from the group, he had noticed the disgusted twist of the enforcer's lips. The shifter cleared his expression swiftly enough, but his scent must have given him away.

Alpha Sturgis inhaled deeply and narrowed his eyes. "I see." Then he nodded at Cassidy before smiling. "Good call, my mate."

Just that fast, the tense set of Cassidy's shoulders eased, and the brown bear shifter smiled back.

"I was told by Alba that her younger sister, Candace, claimed to have met you, and that you were interested in mating with her," Alpha Sturgis explained slowly. "When I told her that there were rumors that you had already taken a male avian shifter as your mate, Alba exploded." Rubbing his hand over his face, he admitted, "She vowed to make you pay for your lies. I told her to leave it, but I didn't stop her when she enlisted the help of her brother." After clearing his throat, Alpha Sturgis told them, "Alba said she'd been in touch with a councilman who was attempting to clean up the council and put a stop to activities that weaken us."

"Did she give you a name?" Vincentius asked.

"Councilman Sasha Delaney," the alpha replied.

Vincentius sighed deeply. "Sasha is no longer on the council."

Frowning, Seever grumbled, "We need a new way to broadcast changes on the council."

"Cho and I have been working on it," Vincentius admitted. Returning his focus to the alpha, he asked, "Did Alba say how she was in contact with Sasha?"

Seever listened as Alpha Sturgis explained how they'd been communicating.

Chapter Twelve

"Hey, Reese! Happy birthday!"

Reese turned and spotted Willow heading into the dining room. "Thanks," he replied warily before returning his focus to the breakfast food he was pulling off his trolley and spreading across the massive buffet table.

Willow chuckled as she stopped next to him and grabbed a plate. "Don't worry. Seever told us that you didn't want a party." She grabbed the spoon and began adding cheesy scrambled eggs onto her plate. "Just know that almost all of us are still going to congratulate you. You're young enough to where it can still be exciting, you see."

"Young enough?" Reese moved the trolley out of her way, so she could reach the sausage links. "What do you mean?"

After licking her fingers, Willow stepped away from the table. "Oh, hon," she teased, her brown eyes twinkling. "You turn thirty-one this year. Just about everyone else around here is at least a century." Rolling her eyes, Willow admitted, "After that many birthdays, friends have a damn tough time coming up with original gifts, so we eventually stop celebrating." As she headed toward the breakfast table, she laughed. "Now we just use it as an excuse to get together and have a few beers."

"You can do that any night," Reese pointed out, feeling a little confused.

Willow nodded. "Exactly."

Reese stared at her for a second, watching her dig into the food he'd provided. It took him a second, but he figured out what she meant. Eventually, birthdays would be just another day.

Turning away, Reese finished refilling what needed it,

then returned to the kitchen. He'd become really good at providing fresh food for every meal. It helped that Thad often gave him a hand and that not everyone ate meals at the same time.

The group going on shift would eat at around seven, then those would be followed by the people who were coming off shift. The many different shifts that started and ended throughout the day meant that he was constantly able to replenish dishes. During lulls, he often prepared casseroles which he would bake the next day or even a few days later.

Both Seever and Vincentius had told Reese that he didn't need to be so hands on. Eventually, Reese might slow down, but he enjoyed being busy. Plus, he was figuring out what people liked and disliked and how to create meals the size needed by a paranormal-heavy estate.

"Reese, hey!" Ashton called, striding into the kitchen. "Happy birthday, man." The American kestrel shifter patted him on the back lightly, then asked, "Is there any of that candy cane creamer left?"

"Candy cane creamer?" Reese slowly shook his head. "I don't remember seeing that in any of the cupboards."

They'd been damn well stocked, too.

"Hon, the candy cane creamer is only available during the holidays," Ranger—Ashton's mate—told him gently, pulling him away from the refrigerator.

Ashton's brows furrowed. "Oh." Then he turned in Ranger's arms and murmured, "But didn't we just celebrate St. Patrick's Day? That's a holiday, isn't it?"

Ranger pressed a gentle kiss to Ashton's lips before murmuring, "It is, my mate. Just the wrong holiday." He winced slightly before explaining, "I'm sorry. I should have said Christmas holiday."

"Oh." Ashton sounded so damn disappointed.

Reese recalled the fact that, even though Ashton was the

alpha of the avian flock living at the councilman's estate, he'd been held in a cage and experimented on for years. He was still learning — or relearning — stuff.

"You know what," Reese mused softly, hating to break into their moment, but he was unable to resist making the offer. "If you're not dead set on coffee, I bet I can give you some tea that'll taste pretty similar."

Ashton turned his attention on him, his expression appearing hopeful. "Really?"

Reese headed to another cupboard as he nodded. "Yeah. With a little doctoring." He grabbed a box from the cupboard and pulled out a tea bag. "This is a spearmint flavored herbal tea," he explained, dropping it into a mug which he'd pulled out of another cupboard. After filling it with steaming water from a carafe on a warming plate, Reese set it on the counter. "Give me just a sec."

Then Reese headed into the pantry. He began glancing around shelves, searching. "I know I saw them when I was doing inventory," he muttered to himself.

"What are you looking for?" Ranger asked, peering into the well-stocked room.

"Ha!" Reese shouted in triumph. He pulled a box from the back and held it up. "Individually wrapped mini candy canes."

Ranger's eyes lit up. "Can I have one?"

"Sure."

Reese pulled out two of them, tossing one to Ranger as he strode past him. The second one, he carefully opened, then placed in the tea mug, resting the crooked end over the side. He picked up the cup, then turned and held it out to Ashton.

"Give it a few minutes to allow the candy cane to melt and the water to cool, then use the cane to stir it," Reese advised, handing it over.

"Thank you." Ashton grinned widely. "I'll give it a shot."

Reese nodded, then began heading toward the stove and the dishes he needed to stir.

Ranger's hand on his shoulder stopped him. "Oh, and we're supposed to send you up to your room. Seever sent us." He winked. "It's your birthday. I think he wants to give you your birthday spankings."

Heat instantly rushed to his cheeks. He swallowed hard as his blood flowed south. Taking a step away from the man, he struggled to think.

Did Seever really tell Ranger and Ashton that I like getting spanked?

Ashton knocked his shoulder into Ranger's, laughing. "Stop freaking Reese out," he ordered before turning a kind smile Reese's way. "He's kidding." Then Ashton rolled his eyes. "About the spankings, anyway. But Seever did ask us to run and get you."

"Why didn't he just call?" Reese asked, relief filling him.

"Couldn't say," Ashton replied. "Now get going. Don't worry about anything else today. The flock's got it covered around the clock."

Reese frowned, but he began pulling off his apron. "Told him not to make a big deal," he grumbled.

"Stop bitchin'," Ranger teased. "Happy birthday, now get the hell out of here."

After handing off his apron, Reese headed out of the kitchen. He took a second to flip the jackal shifter off, just for good measure. Except, all that earned him was the sound of both men's laughter.

Stalking through the estate, Reese thought about all the things he would do to his man when he reached his suite. Still, every time he passed someone and they wished him a happy birthday, he couldn't stop the slight warmth that settled in his belly.

Everyone here is just so damn nice.

Reese opened the door to the suite he shared with Seever.

Just a month before, if someone had told him he would fall in love and move in with a wealthy, white guy, he would have laughed in his face . . . or maybe decked him.

God, I was an ass.

After closing the door, Reese called for his lover.

"In the bedroom, babe," Seever hollered back.

Reese grinned.

Birthday spankings, indeed.

His dick thickened just at the thought. His asshole also clenched, and his gut churned, butterflies tumbling. Still, he resisted the urge to strip his clothes.

Turning the corner, Reese froze in the doorway to the bedroom. He rested his hands on either side of the frame as he gaped at the view. His heart rate spiked in his chest, and drool pooled in his mouth.

"Hey, babe," Seever greeted, his voice husky. "Happy birthday." He waved his hand toward his hard dick, which jutted up from his groin . . . and it was wrapped with a bow made of red ribbon. "I thought perhaps you'd like to unwrap your gift early." Seever waggled his brows as he next indicated the nightstand. "If you're upset, I bet a little cake would sweeten you up."

Reese had trouble yanking his gaze away from Seever's be-ribboned dick. He wanted to pull the damn thing off with his tongue. Glancing toward the nightstand, he snorted a laugh.

There sat a cake that looked just like Seever's erection. Even the tannish icing gave it a similar appearance. Some kind of red candy filament was wrapped around it in a bow.

"My, my, my . . ." Reese finally managed to get out. He reached down and rubbed his dick through his jeans. "What wonderful options." As he spoke, he popped the button on his fly, then slowly lowered the zipper. "Whatever should I choose?"

"I'm sure I don't know," Seever stated on a growl while

lowering his hand to tease along the base of his erection. "Better choose fast though, or I'm gonna take the choice away from you."

Reese grinned, then whipped his polo shirt over his head. Once again meeting Seever's eyes, he dropped the shirt on the floor as he waggled his finger. "Now, now. Don't be impatient. It's *my* birthday, after all."

"Yes, it is," Seever murmured, his whiskey-brown eyes smoldering.

Sucking in a surprised breath, Reese realized that was the first time he'd used his birthday in a lighthearted way in . . . a long damn time. His heart suddenly felt light. As he peered at his naked lover, Reese realized it was all due to the gorgeous specimen of maleness that lay sprawled and needy on the bed.

"I love you," Reese whispered.

Seever sucked in a harsh breath. His brows shot up. Then, an instant later, Seever's eyes began to gleam, and a wide grin split his lips.

"I love you, too, Reese." Then he again beckoned with his fingers. "Now get over here."

Reese loved the desire, the need that he saw glowing from Seever's eyes. In fact, he wanted to see more of it. Humming, he rested his thumbs into the top of his jeans, then pushed them down and off.

Straightening, Reese caught his breath in his throat. "God, you are so handsome," he mumbled. Upon seeing Seever's wide smile, he grinned back, ignoring the heat on his cheeks.

"So," Reese murmured as he slowly rounded the bed. All the while, he teased his prick, sliding his fingers up and down his cock lightly. "My choice." Stopping at the nightstand, he leered at Seever. "I know what you normally taste like. What about this?"

Moving his hands to his ass, Reese pulled apart his ass

cheeks as he bent at the waist. When he heard Seever's long, low groan, he knew his lover had spotted his own birthday surprise. Reese was wearing a butt plug.

Reese cast a flirty glance over his shoulder, admiring Seever's flushed cheeks and dilated eyes—not to mention the bead of pre-cum gleaming from the tip of his erection. Returning his focus to the penis cake, he stuck out his tongue and took a slow swipe up from base to tip. The sweet buttercream frosting burst on his tongue, then mixed with the cinnamon-flavored bows caused his taste buds to sing.

"Mmmmm." Reese peered over his shoulder as he licked his lips exaggeratedly. "Yummy."

It really was good, too. He loved buttercream frosting and cinnamon separately, but both was fantastic.

Seever growled at him, baring his teeth. His need was visible in every line of his face.

"Want some?" Reese did his best to sound innocent.

"Yessss," Seever hissed.

With a wink, Reese returned to the penis cake. He licked it twice more, then straightened. Gripping the base of his dick, he rocked his hips forward and swiped his crown up the length, scooping up a bit of frosting and candied ribbon.

Then Reese carefully turned and faced the bed.

Seever moaned and licked his lips. The bead of pre-cum grew bigger, sliding off his crown to drop onto his abdominals. He didn't seem to notice, for his focus remained riveted on Reese's dick.

"Please," Seever whispered.

Reese let out a groan of his own, having never heard his big, dominant lover beg before. Ever-so-carefully, he climbed onto the bed, then slowly knee-walked forward. Once he was close enough, he eased onto all fours over Seever's head, allowing his throbbing shaft to dangle toward his lover's lips.

Seever wasted no time. Opening his mouth, he lifted his head. He wrapped his lips around Reese's dick head and suckled lightly. At the same time, he swiped his tongue back and forth over his head, cleaning him and teasing his sensitive flesh.

Reese's ass clenched, causing the plug in his chute to shift. It slid across his prostate, yanking a hiss from his throat. When Seever reached up and slid his fingertips along his ball sack, his breathing was reduced to harsh pants.

Peering down at Seever, Reese watched his lover suck his dick and play with his testicles. He spread his legs wider, unable to help himself. Seever took that as an invitation. His lover met his gaze even as he skimmed a fingertip along his crease. When he reached Reese's plug, he jostled it gently, sending cascades of stimulus through his rectum.

Panting harshly, Reese rocked between the touches. His hips jerked spastically, and he felt his balls tingle. Knowing his orgasm neared, he attempted to lift up.

Seever must have read his intent, for he snaked his free arm around Reese's waist, quick as a flash, holding him in place. Pulling him closer, his lover sucked him deeper. At the same time, he began smacking his ass.

The sting coupled with the jiggle of the plug in his ass set his balls on fire. Reese arched and screamed. His orgasm crashed over him, sending his senses soaring.

Twitches continued to besiege Reese's body as he floated on the endorphins of his release. He eventually became conscious of Seever's light rubs over his overly stimulated butt cheeks. Reese welcomed the pleasure-pain and hummed appreciatively.

Finally, Seever turned his head, allowing Reese's half-hard prick to slip from his mouth. "Mmmm," he murmured. "You, buttercream, and cinnamon." He grinned lasciviously. "Exquisite."

Reese could only grin, since his brain was still offline.

"Now open your present, Reese," Seever urged, sliding his fingertip around his stretched hole. "Do it now, my love."

Moaning, Reese did as he was urged, even though his limbs felt damn uncoordinated. He eased sideways until his mouth was hovering near Seever's dick. Lowering his head and opening his mouth, he carefully gripped the end of the ribbon between his teeth.

Then, oh-so-slowly, Reese pulled.

The ribbon untwined, and Reese discovered it was wound in such a way that it slowly slipped free of his dick. He loved the long, low growl that erupted from his lover's throat. It told him that Seever enjoyed the stimulation of the velvety ribbon sliding over his hard flesh.

When Reese was done, it was his turn to gasp.

Seever eased the butt plug from his chute so slowly that he had to clench his teeth to keep from snapping at the man.

"Now, then," Seever murmured huskily. "Turn around and climb aboard."

Reese did as he was told and swung his leg over Seever's waist. Anticipation thrummed through him as he watched his lover position his dick between them. Obeying the urging of Seever's other hand, which he'd moved to Reese's hip, he began to sink down . . . down. Feeling the pressure of Seever's crown at his entrance, he pushed out and kept going.

Once Reese was settled fully on Seever's erection, he paused and let out a deep sigh.

"Gods, that is a gorgeous look on you," Seever whispered.

Blinking open eyelids that Reese hadn't realized he'd closed, he grinned down at Seever. "Oh, yeah?"

Upon seeing Seever's loving smile, an answering surge of happiness flooded Reese.

"Yeah, babe." Seever wrapped his arms around Reese and pulled him forward. "Kiss me."

Reese went happily along with that notion. As his lips met Seever's, he felt his shifter slide his palm to his still-tingling ass. A shiver worked through Reese as their tongues dueled together.

Seever urged him to start moving, lifting and lowering in slow, measured movements. All the while they made out, and Reese couldn't remember the last time he'd had such an amazing birthday.

You may also enjoy the following from eXtasy Books Inc:

With a Wolf's Support
Charlie Richards

Excerpt

Leo tightened his leather trench coat around himself, shoving his hands into his pockets. He squinted against the wind as he watched the helicopter land on the pad which was situated over a hundred yards behind Manon's home. Hunching his shoulders, he did his best to ignore the chill.

A few seconds after the whirly-bird had landed, the whine of the engine softened, and the rotors began to slow. He watched the door open, and Manon slipped out, ducking under the still-churning blades. The wolf shifter enforcer jogged toward him, nodding in greeting.

"Give me ten minutes. I gotta run in and piss, then grab a sandwich and water. Stow your stuff and strap it down, will ya?" Then he winked and added, "Also gonna kiss my man and tell him how much I miss him."

Leo was still nodding when Manon disappeared down the trail.

"Stow my stuff," Leo muttered under his breath. He'd never been in a helicopter but still. "How hard could it be?"

Leo took his time figuring it out.

To Leo's surprise, he enjoyed his first helicopter ride. With his superior shifter eyesight, even though it was night, he could make out quite a bit of what was below them. The sensation of soaring through the air was almost as enjoyable as running through the forest in wolf form—almost.

"I see why you learned how to fly one of these," Leo called over the rumble of the engine. "This is fun."

Manon glanced his way for an instant before returning his focus to the controls. "Yep. Did Alpha Declan fill you in?"

Leo nodded. "For the most part."

"Good." Manon chuckled darkly. "That way we don't have to shout back and forth the whole ride."

Laughing, Leo returned his focus to the darkness outside.

They reached the airport a little after three in the morning. As Leo relaxed in the passenger seat of the SUV that Manon drove—he'd offered, but the enforcer had told him it would be easier for him to drive since he knew the way—he noticed the illuminated bank sign reading two-twelve AM.

Right. We gained an hour.

They drove through surprisingly still-crowded streets. Cars honked, tires squealed, and the music from other vehicles thumped as they passed them. That was something Leo sure didn't miss. Living in the country offered a much quieter, sedate lifestyle that, as a wolf shifter, Leo craved.

And a mate.

Leo had been watching all his friends, and even his family, find their mates for years. At almost two hundred years old, he would love to finally find someone to call his own. His patience was wearing thin, so he sure hoped Fate hurried the fuck up.

"Wow, nice houses," Leo commented, staring out the window and admiring the mansions, hoping to distract himself from his wayward thoughts.

"Well, as it turns out, Jared refuses to stay in anything but the finest." Manon smiled wryly as he glanced Leo's way. "And of course Carson isn't going to do a damn thing to counter his mate."

Laughing softly, Leo murmured, "Yeah."

Leo didn't spend a lot of time with most of the wolves of the inner circle. With his duties of monitoring the length of time the adults in their pack had lived as a certain identity, he spent a lot of time with everyone else in the pack. In the past, Leo had sent his reports, which contained his recommendations of who should soon consider a change, to Beta Shane Alvaro.

Since Beta Shane had moved on to take a position on the Shifter Council, Leo had begun sending the reports to Alpha Declan himself. Even though they'd held a challenge — which was won by a big, dominant, blond wolf shifter named Dixon Holsteen — so a new beta had been assigned, Leo hadn't yet been given the word to send the reports to him. From what Leo had heard, Alpha Declan was still easing him into his myriad of duties.

One of those would eventually be working with Leo to coordinate with the shifters in their pack to change their identities. In order to do that, however, Dixon had to know everyone in the pack. He had to meet them, learn about who they were, how long they'd been in the pack, and absorb the complexity of their relationships around them.

Seeing as Leo already knew the information, he didn't envy Dixon the process.

It was a lot to take in.

The same as nearly everyone in the pack who could get the day off of work, Leo had been at the Right for Position challenge. He'd seen the dominant shifters fight. It'd been damn impressive, and Leo had been glad he would never be pitted against any of them — gods willing. While his wolf was fairly dominant, it took a certain aggressiveness to want to fight for a top position.

Leo just didn't have it.

"This is it." Manon's voice cut into Leo's thoughts. "You awake over there?"

Jerking his focus back to the wolf enforcer, Leo took in the lines of tension etched on Manon's face. "I'm awake. Was just lost in thought," he admitted, turning his attention to the house—mansion—they were approaching. "Took a nap earlier," he admitted. "Now I'm ready to check on my family before finding a bed. I bet you're ready to crash, though."

"You know it."

The gate opened before them, and Manon steered the vehicle down the long driveway and past gorgeous landscaping. Leo spotted the house and found himself smirking. When Carson's mate said he wanted nice digs to rescue people and take out some drug gangs, he wasn't kidding. Of course, Leo had to admit that since they were within a fenced estate, it had to help with safety, too.

As their vehicle approached, the garage door on the far-left side opened. Manon parked them inside the cavernous space. Once the other shifter turned off the engine, Leo pushed out of the vehicle, closing the door behind him. He opened the back door and grabbed his bags. After slinging his suit bag over his shoulder, Leo used his hip to close the door, then he followed Manon across the garage toward a door on the far end.

Manon used a key to unlock it, then opened it and led the way inside.

Leo stepped into a large foyer and waited as Manon closed and locked the door behind him. Following the other shifter once more, he was led through a back hallway. He pointed toward the far end, explaining that it led to a back foyer.

"Here's the main hall," Manon murmured softly, opening a door and stepping through. He pointed toward the stairs to the right, saying, "I'm supposed to take you to Alpha Declan first, though. He said he'd still be up."

Even as Leo nodded, a scent tickled his senses, distracting him. He turned to the left as he inhaled more deeply. A mossy, earthy fragrance somehow mixed with a natural male aroma. It left his taste buds tingling and his mouth watering.

Needing to discern the source, Leo set his bags down on a nearby settee. While he figured it was a piece of furniture that was probably only for decoration, Leo didn't care. Parsing out the source of the exquisite aroma . . . that was all that mattered.

"Leo?" Manon called. "Where are you going?"

"I need—" Leo glanced over his shoulder and spotted Manon's questioning expression. "What's this way?"

"The kitchen and dining areas."

Nodding absently, Leo picked up his pace. Anticipation flooded him, and his breathing quickened. Even his wolf grew excited in his mind.

Leo pushed open a door and peered around, taking in a small, dark dining room. His keen eyesight surveyed a bar separating the space, which led into a huge kitchen. His gaze fixated on a young man standing frozen before the open door of the refrigerator, his form silhouetted in the light.

Sucking in a harsh breath, Leo could only stare. The human was, in a word, stunning. He appeared lean—easily seen even hidden beneath a pair of loose-fitting sleep pants and a t-shirt—and stood perhaps five-foot-eight or nine. I'll have to get closer to be sure. His hair gleamed red in the light of the refrigerator, wild and unkempt.

Even while admiring all that, Leo noticed the male's wide, wide green eyes . . . eyes full of trepidation and fear.

Why? What's wrong?

Leo longed to soothe the man, and the reason why hit him hard.

He's my mate!

Leo swallowed convulsively, forcing moisture into his mouth. "Damn. Fate listened," he whispered.

Manon lifted a brow, his expression one of confusion. "What are you talking about?"

Unable to tear his gaze away from the svelte, red-haired figure staring at them with that wide-eyed, fearful look, Leo felt another stab of need to ease the tension filling the human's frame. "He's my mate."

About the Author

Charlie started writing fantasy when she was eight, and after stumbling onto her first erotic romance at age nineteen, she realized her true calling. She now focuses on writing gay erotic romance, normally of the paranormal variety, with heroes of all kinds. With the help and support of her husband, Charlie finally fulfilled one of her life-long goals . . . move to acreage with her horses. You can often find her curled up with her laptop and a cup of tea or glass of wine, creating her next adventure. Charlie enjoys exploring the mountains of her new Oregon home on horseback, 4-wheeler, or motorcycle.

She can be reached at ch.richards2010@yahoo.com

Or visit her at www.charlie-richards.com.

www.ingramcontent.com/pod-product-compliance
Lightning Source LLC
Chambersburg PA
CBHW060644130626
46555CB00002B/945